The True Story of Queen Victoria's Indian Servant Amongst Other Matters

The True Story of Queen Victoria's Indian Servant

Amongst Other Matters

Tony Lester

Published in 2013 by FeedARead Publishing
Copyright © Tony Lester.
British Library C.I.P.
A CIP catalogue record for this title is available from
the British Library.

Author's Note

I was on my way to Kingston from Surbiton where I intended to do some shopping when I saw a skip outside a large Victorian house in Anglesea Road. I looked into it. After all, I had been lucky on a previous occasion when I rescued some one-hundred year-old rafters that were now adorning my garden having been converted into a garden arch. In one corner of the skip I saw some old newspapers that were terribly stained. I looked at one that was dated 3rd March 1902. It was not only stained but torn and and covered in brick dust that made it difficult to read but I persevered as a workman came along with a barrow. I was pleased to see that he had a unlit cigarette end hanging from the corner of his mouth and was not wearing a face mask, both facts I knew would add a certain verisimilitude to my story if I ever had to tell how I found a Ming jar in a skip.

"You all right?" he said. He had come out of the house to throw more rubbish into the skip.

"Yes", I replied. "Can I take anything I find away?"

"Yes Guvnor. Help yourself. It's all rubbish that we're clearing out of the attic so we can build an extension. You won't find any hairlooms there."

He coughed and lit the cigarette. I thought that he really should be wearing a mask but decided not to give him that advice, nor the figures on cancer that came from smoking.

4

"Nor any antiques for that antique show", added a better dressed man who joined us.

"Well if you're quite sure..."

"Look, I'm the gaffer on this job, so if say it's OK it's OK."
"But the people who are paying you..."

" ...have said they want all the rubbish cleared out. Every thing."

I pulled what seemed to be a bundle of newspapers bound together with some string from under a pile of old mortar. I looked at the gaffer. Before I could say another word the gaffer said irritably:

"Yes, go on take them. They are only bloody old newspapers. You can take the others if you want but as you can see they are all stained and rotten from the leak that we found."

I slipped my bundle into a plastic bag, the sort that you can buy in a supermarket and then renew it when it wears out. I abandoned my walk and went home instead. My shopping could wait. I was looking forward instead to looking through my bundle of papers. They were not a Ming vase and they might just be rubbish to the builders but to me they were a link with the past that would give me lots of pleasure as I sorted them out. I also knew some historians in Surbiton who might equally be interested in seeing them.

When I examined my find I discovered that it was not a bundle of newspapers at all but several newspapers that were dated 1902 that were wrapped around something. I cut the string and unfolded the papers to find a solid block of papers that were covered in the most beautiful copperplate handwriting. As I looked at page after page I realised that I was looking at a manuscript of some kind. After looking at the first few pages I carefully wrapped up all the papers, and the following day I went back to the house. The skip was gone. A bent grey-haired man cutting the hedge nearby came over to join me.

"You looking for those cowboys? They've scarpered. I knew they were wrong uns. You can always tell."

No, he didn't know who owned the house, and the local authority when I approached them were even more unhelpful than usual, so I thought I would simply regard my find as a gift from the gods. And what a gift it proved to be. Now that I have transcribed it onto my computer and re-arranged it somewhat, you too can decide how lucky I was, for it has turned out to be a complete book in embryo! All it really lacked was a title. As you see I have given it one, but I doubt that it does the story full justice.

PART ONE

How It All Began

Chapter 1

1866

The Moving Finger writes; and, having writ,
Moves on: nor all thy Piety nor Wit
Shall lure it back to cancel half a Line,
Nor all thy Tears wash out a Word of it.

There was no sound of a crash, just a silence that was more menacing than any noise. The workman called out anxiously to his mate, then as he got no answer he went round to the other side of the wagon to where they were engaged in shunting it. He found William Bollen sitting next to the track pale and listless. When he got William up William walked with his hand held to the side of his neck.

"They pinched me. They pinched me. I am likely to die from it; I know I shall. Oh the pain."

He slid down and his shunting pole rolled away. Charlie Freeman said:

"Pinched you? How did they do that? Who pinched you?"

"I don't know. Give us a drink of brandy for God's sake."

The brandy seemed to revive him. Some colour came back into his cheeks. His neck was bright red. He stood up suddenly. Then, just as suddenly he slowly sank down and a mixture of brandy and blood came out of his mouth. He fell back. The doctor, when he came at last, having been called away from his dinner, was curt.

"He's dead."

He wiped his hands on the napkin that he had brought with him from the dinner table and went back to the cab that had brought him. Charlie followed him saying:

"But why is he dead? What killed him."

"I don't know. The coroner will say though once there has been a post mortem."

He climbed into the cab and the cabbie said:

"Walk on", without being told that the doctor wanted to go home to his interrupted dinner.

The proceedings in the Antelope public house in Surbiton were not exactly rushed, but then they were not either unduly lingered over. After all it was fairly clear that this was just another railway accident, one of many that were seemingly inevitable as railways grew and lines were expanded. Just as they ate up tons of steel so did they consume, alongside a diet of railway lines, a measure of human flesh. The authorities were of the opinion that it was simply the men's fault; were they to take more care then the accidents would not happen so often.

No notice was taken of the fact that so many of the accidents happened at the end of a shift when the men were at their lowest ebb, having been at work so long. So once again a verdict was given of: "accidental death".   Mrs Bollen, William Bollen's wife accepted the verdict stoically. It was one that she had expected. She had been told that because of the strange circumstances of the death she would be given a payment and was pleased to hear that. Later on she was not so pleased when the money that was given her was a mere ten pounds. Of course that amount was what many a housemaid was paid for a year's work, but they were also kept, fed and given clothing. Luckily she had only the one child, a girl, so she could stretch the money, but eventually it would run out. It looked as if she would have to go back into service. She did so and I was her employer. That was in 1866 when I came on leave from India.

My name is Manfred Driscoll, a name that you will probably never have heard of. Indeed I would be astonished if my name meant anything at all to you. You will certainly know the name of our late Queen, Queen Victoria whose funeral you either attended in 1891 or read about, or were told of, if you cannot read. Did you know by the way that she was actually called Alexandrina Victoria, but insisted on dropping the name Alexandrina when she came to the throne and just kept the name Victoria? I expect you did not. So many facts are lost or forgotten or hidden away. Perhaps you were one of those poor children who were assembled in Hyde Park to sing 'God Save the Queen' when she had her Golden Jubilee. I wonder if you still have the little pot that had the picture of Her Majesty on it that they gave you? Somehow I doubt it, but perhaps it's still on the mantelpiece holding spills to light the gas. Do people still roll pieces of newspaper to make spills? Will everyone know how India was saved to continue as the jewel in the queen's crown? It all depends upon whether my story that I have set down ever gets published.

So many facts are lost or forgotten or hidden away, rather like those little pots. My story reveals some of the real facts that were also hidden away that were behind that business over the Queen's Munshi, and I am writing it so that in future when all the persons concerned are dead the truth can safely be told. I flatter myself that I am not a vain man but would like others to know more of myself and how I was part of what was possibly an important moment in our history.

Historians try to tell you what really happened in the past. They are obliged to use written material in the main: official reports, diaries, letters, books and so on. All these sources are suspect of course, and historians would be the first to admit this. Official reports frequently reflect what the organisation that commissioned them wish to hear. Diaries are necessarily tainted by selection; no one can include everything and what is included depends upon the diarists' interests, not to mention their subjective accounts. Letters are better in some way, particularly if they are hand written, but they must be read in context. As to books, why did the writer choose to write about this particular matter that is the subject of the book, and how many mistakes has he or she made, let alone the bias inherent in the selection of material. Of course academic rigour can overcome a great deal of the problems of getting at the truth.

A particular problem exists however when we come to the role of the secret police in any country or state. Throughout history the secret police have existed, and as their activities are secret it follows that any attempt to discover how they operated and what they actually did is going to be difficult. It is axiomatic that their activities and policies are hidden; this is necessary if their work is to be successful, particularly if they are coping with threats, real or imagined, from other countries.

But in time if the threat no longer exists their work no longer needs to be protected. It becomes possible to tell all (well not quite all). And the person who can tell you most will be the one who was in the secret police. I think therefore that I can tell the world what really happened when Queen Victoria seemed to become obsessed with her Indian Servant, her Munshee, for I mean to set it all down for some one to publish if they see fit when I and all the others who were involved are dead.

Now I know that having warned you about the limitations of what has been written down being the real truth you will probably ask why you should not be equally wary of what you are about to read. Please, I beg of you, retain that wariness. As you read my account measure it against other accounts, and above all ask yourself what do I gain by telling my story from my perspective?

And just before I go any further I have to admit that the little scenario that I used to get your interest at the beginning of my account owes a little something to my imagination. I was not actually there when the events that are set out took place. I can nevertheless vouch for most of the facts for, as you will read, always supposing that I have captured your attention sufficiently to ensure that you do indeed read what I have so laboured to produce, I had an honest and steadfast witness. What follows now however is a story that is completely true and explains with some precision the truth behind the late Queen

Victoria and her munshi or moonshi. It's an Indian word so translates into either spelling.

In order to do so I have to go back to the time when I first met James Sleeman. It is necessary I can assure you for unless I do so I cannot fully explain what really happened. Now you might just have heard something of that man and how he dealt with Thuggee in India? If you have not I suggest that you read 'Confessions of a Thug' by Meadows Taylor. I know it's a bit of a shocker, but it's written by a first rate British Officer who was stationed in India so he knows what he is writing about. In my opinion Sleeman deserves to be much better known. I am biased of course as I met him and worked with him and admired his achievements immensely.

I started as many others did at the East India Company Military Seminary at Addiscombe, Surrey. There was a similar institution in Hertfordshire. That was where clerks started their careers. You can imagine how we in the Military Seminary despised them. I was there for two years and then went to India. I will not bore you with my travails on that journey. Sufficient to say that I was immensely pleased when it was over. A certain young woman who appears later on in this account suffered more than I did, so who am I to complain?

Chapter 2

1835

Alas, that Spring should vanish with the Rose!
That Youth's sweet-scented Manuscript should close!
The Nightingale that in the Branches sang,
Ah, whence, and whither flown again, who knows!

Why do I venerate Sleeman so much? It's not just his work in dealing with Thuggee, but what happened to me when I was first in India. I was griffin when I arrived in India in 1835. That's the nickname that was given to any new recruit to the East India Company. Don't ask me why. Well, all such lads are seen as a source of amusement to all the old hands in India. They all inevitably make mistakes that provide diversion for everyone, but alongside this amusement there is a darker side. Because of their inexperience they are taken advantage of. Practically everyone joins in the fun of exploiting the naivety of the new arrivals and relieving them of little money came with. What is worse is the way some of them are seduced into debts that take some clearing.

When I arrived at the dock at Calcutta clutching a soldered metal case and with a roped wooden box that contained such things as my mother decreed were necessary to my future existence (including woollen vests that I never wore but nevertheless turned out to be extremely useful) I was immediately set on by two black men. They were practically naked as they wore more cloth wound about their heads than they had around their loins. The smiled encouragingly at me as they threw my case and box into a donga.

"Please to get in sahib ", I was entreated. I did so, but as I entered the smelly vehicle my case and box were being removed by two other villainous looking chaps from the other side. My two original blacks let out a great shout of 'Thieves! Robbers', and wrestled to get back my gear. Eventually, when a crowd had gathered to see the fun, my gear was put back into the donga and the thieves ran off. I was then taken along the front away from the crowd where the driver looked round menacingly and demanded that I should pay him right away as I had been saved from being robbed. I had been warned that the niggers would try to gull me so I stood my ground and refused to pay.

At this point the thieves returned and the whole band stood there grinning and thinking, no doubt, that they had me. It looked as if my career was coming to an end before I had even got it started.

"Hullo. What's this?" said a very English voice and I turned in relief to see a man who I later found out to be Sleeman himself who had been coming to the docks to meet someone. Of course I did not know who he was at that time and only found out later. It was extremely fortunate that he was there at all for normally he was totally occupied in ????

He immediately sized up the situation and let rip with a torrent of what I took to be Hindustani. The effect was wonderful. In no time at all the donga was turned around and I was taken to Basaret where the college was situated. This was where I was to finish my training. Here Sleeman told me exactly how much I was to pay. I was of a mind to tell them to whistle for their money but he told me that it was imperative that I paid my way correctly.

"They may be badmashes, but you are British so you are better than they, and must accordingly act so."

Is it any wonder that I thought William Sleeman was wonderful? Never mind about Ganesh, Kali or Shiva, I had met my own personal God that day. It was only in the latter part of that year that I found that in the very year that I came to India he went on a journey to recover his health; he had apparently worked so hard that was thoroughly debilitated.

Much later on as I rose, mainly through my efforts to understand the customs, language and the people I was drawn into his orbit where I worked on putting down such remnants of thuggee that still existed. When we were not doing so we dealt with dacoits.

In the meantime as you might expect I read as much as I could about the way that thugee had been dealt with. I was impressed at the way that thugs who became informers could be used to incriminate their previous associates. They were called 'approvers' and were immediately set to work; in some cases going by night to where they knew a thug was living so that he could be arrested. On more than one occasion the arrested thug immediately offered to be an approver, for the way they regarded their work meant that if it was necessary to switch allegiance they would do so with no hesitation at all.

In time it became possible to assume that we had pretty well rid the country of this terrible blight. Most of the thugs were incarcerated in prison, and indeed I can say that many were to stay there until they died there. It may sound awfully harsh but against their lack of freedom must be set the terrible consequences of what they did: widows were left unsupported; children were orphaned and, quite shocking to me, a number of sepoys who had been on their way home with their pitifully small amounts of money that they had garnered in their service to John Company had been murdered. You might think that I should not place the lives of soldiers above those of civilians, but if it became widely known that these guardians of law and order were not immune to attacks from thugs then all confidence would be lost in British administration.

You have to remember how extremely small were our numbers and how spread out we were. Although we did not at the time that I went out to India rule over all of it, we nevertheless occupied a considerable part.   If we could not maintain some semblance of civilized government in those parts then we were lost.   Actually it did get to the point that we overcame thuggee so well that the Thuggee and Dacoity Department had to find other activities in order to continue its existence.   I will say nothing of the Criminal Tribes Act of 1876 as it is not part of my story except, as you will see, how the department went on afterwards to get involved in a much wider range of activities. But just as ridding India of thuggee was so important, so was dealing with all other sorts of nastiness; and it fell to the white man to do this for the blacks had long since given up any attempt do so.

By the time that I was in India Sleeman had carried out such an enormous programme of arrests that many thought that thuggee had been eradicated. This was not so, for just as in the beginning when Sleeman uncovered the wide scale of thuggee and magistrates were unbelieving that such villainy could be so wide-spread without their knowledge, they now swung to the opposite view of admitting that it was everywhere, but had now been totally put down. I was to encounter that it still existed myself, and indeed on one notable occasion when I rode out to follow up what we had been told by an informer we actually arrested several thugs.

Chapter 3

1838

Folk of a surly Tapster tell
"And daub his Visage with the Smoke of Hell;
"They talk of some strict Testing of us---Pish!
"He's a Good Fellow, and 't will all be well."

Religion is everywhere in India you know. No matter what time of the day year or month it is; no matter where you are, North, South, East or West, or who you are, for that matter, you cannot avoid it. And it is all tremendously exciting. It's colourful, noisy and so uninhibited. Some of the blacks, the niggers, go totally nude, begging your pardon, but after the first shock you don't see the nakedness. What you see is sheer exuberance, total vitality with people declaring their beliefs in activity. It's all totally captivating. I never tired of watching the great festivals; watching a horde of totally naked men daubed with gaudy colours and waving tridents as they rush into the Ganges is a sight to behold. Not one for the ladies, of course! Although, as you will read later there was a woman in my story who declined to accept the traditional notions of morality and enjoyed the sight that I have described above for what it was: an exhibition of religious fervour. Well, I do hope that was the reason why she enjoyed it.

I immediately resolved that, apart from what I was expected to learn, I would devote myself to studying all the splendid riotous religions that were going on about me full tilt. In point of fact I pride myself on the fact that I had already mastered most of what I was expected to learn at Addiscombe so was pretty well perfect when it came to drill and such stuff, so I had time to devote to other pursuits. I avoided going out to shoot fowl and I tried to keep my carousing to a minimum. I was expected to learn some languages, and I did so easily. My ease in capturing the various native tongues and dialects brought me instant recognition. Unfortunately it also earned me a reputation that was to cause me as much trouble as it brought me promotion. Behind my back I was called a nigger lover. I was more than once accused of 'going native'. This was following several sorties on my part into those areas where white men seldom ventured.

Others did, but they were seeking sexual gratification rather than knowledge. I can tell you this for you must have some ideas of the ways that young men might seek to divert themselves when they do not have the restraining influence of a loving wife and marriage. Of course a Christian upbringing should have been useful to them too in resisting temptation, but alas, many of them seemed to think that having left England behind them that meant they could also leave their inhibitions as well.

What assisted me in resisting such temptations was my experience on the dance floor. Although ensigns, and even captains, were not considered much of a catch by women who were on the lookout for a husband, they were nevertheless invited to all sorts of social occasions including dances. Now, although I am able to sit a horse and march about in uniform, when it comes to quadrilles, gavottes, the waltz and similar how d'ye dos, I seem to have two left feet. So I was quickly dropped from the list of young men to be invited. Not that I was worried. In fact I was pleased as it meant that I could spend more time on finding out about the various religious beliefs and honing my languages. I even managed a smattering of Ramasee, which is strictly speaking a thieves cant, not a language at all. It was what the thugs spoke to each other when going about their deadly business as they did not want to let their intended victims know what they were up to.

As to getting involved with a native woman, I avoided all that. In time I heard from 'old hands' who 'knew the ropes' that in the past there were many who came out from England to join the Company, took a mistress and never went home; they simply made India their home. At the same time by having children they created a whole intermediate group of people who were neither English nor Indian. At first these offspring were accepted. It was only much later that they began to be shunned.

I did have a friend, a woman who was one of those unfortunates whose unattractiveness was so apparent that no matter how she might dress or have her hair curled she was, as I heard one of her more fortunate sisters styled her, 'a fright'. Joan Biddlesworth was the unmarried sister of Eve Frobert-Frobisher who was married to Captain George Frobert-Frobisher. She was in India as an act of charity for everyone accepted that that, given her sturdy frame, very homely features and, most important of all, no fortune, she was unlikely ever to achieve marital status. At balls and other similar events when I first made her acquaintance the poor girl would sit miserably in a corner.

In England as a maiden aunt she would have led a similar life. I have since met many of her kind. Useful souls, often the backbone of the households where there was money. Where there was none, or very little, they were tolerated, sometimes with affection but more often with exasperation or even bitterness. I imagine that were these women ever to write novels they would have a perfect subject immediately to hand: their own lives.

With my wooden feet that so stubbornly refused to accept my orders and left me looking a fool on the dance floor I too sought a quiet corner until everyone learned not to invite me to such events, and so I met Joan. At first our conversation consisted of those topics deemed respectable enough for persons of our age and standing. Joan was never allowed the compliment of needing a chaperone. Indeed I rather fancy that her brother in law would not have been not too upset were his ugly duckling sister in law to be compromised. I heard that he even cavilled at paying for an ayah for her! This meant that inevitably our conversation became much more interesting for I discovered that Joan, deprived of the sort of life enjoyed by her female companions, was an avid reader. She told me once that she was reading 'The Improvisantore', a book that I had not even heard of, let alone read. It was written by a Danish chap, Hans Christian Andersen, whose name meant nothing to me. I do not suppose for a single moment that you have heard of him either.

I told her that I thought that I might have found that she would have preferred to read something by an English author. She smiled and told me that she also had some books written by a lady. Of course, she said, they are not about politics or wars nor any of the really serious subjects. Instead they look at what life is like for a woman. Initially I accepted this but as I came to know Joan better I wondered if she was not having a joke at my expense.

Now you might ask: what about my own religious beliefs, were they not challenged by what I saw? Did I not think as you saw these poor heathens that they were all damned as they had not been brought to the true love of Christ? Did I not consider that it was my duty as a Christian to turn them from their idolatry, never mind how exciting and interesting it was to me?"

Well, you know, I was brought up in a strict sect where enjoyment was looked upon suspiciously. Sober behaviour was held out as the way in which men and women should comport themselves, so I suppose that when I was faced with religions where people enjoyed themselves as they worshipped it made me wonder about my own beliefs. Do remember that these, so-called heathens, had been practising their religions for long before we ever went to India; and I must say that many of them practised a humanity that challenged what some of my, so called civilised colleagues did.

Anyway, to continue, my language studies gave me many opportunities to question my teachers about their religious beliefs. At first they were suspicious. Why was I so interested? Was this the precursor to a ban upon some of their practises? Was it a subtle way for me to worm my way into their confidence so that I could try to convert them? Christian Missionaries were known for their trickery that they excused by saying that: " To tell a lie is a sin, but a greater sin is to refuse to lie to save a sinner."

Knowing the languages of the natives also helped me from being defrauded by them. I saw some of my companions in arms who seemed to have turned their faces from any form of learning other than that forced on them by being in John Company. As a consequence their servants no only defrauded them but even stole their belongings. Now, as you might imagine, because I turned away from shooting and drinking (well I must admit I did some of that) and pressed on with my language studies I often heard things said by the niggers that they had no idea I understood. I was laying down the foundations of my future career without realising it.

In time as I gained their trust and developed some ability in Hindustani and other tongues, they relaxed, opened up, and eventually offered to take me where Europeans normally did not go. In so doing I made an enormous jump in my knowledge; I also gained two loyal and devoted servants: Raj Dal and Mamoud Patel. Unfortunately at this precise time I also made a formidable enemy in Thomas Forbes-Bosely who was a distant relative of Henry Paget, the second Earl of Uxbridge and First Marquess of Anglesey. This latter fact was not only known by everyone, for Thomas Forbes-Bosely made sure that everyone knew it, but greatly increased the danger of my having him as an enemy.

Like me he had come to India, but unlike me he was the scion of a well-connected family and he used this, and his relationship with The Marquess of Anglesey quite shamelessly to gain favour and promotion. While I diligently learned about the customs and languages of the natives, he cultivated those influential families who formed the top echelons of the East India Company. Consequently in any situation where there might be any doubt about what had happened or what had been said, it was always Thomas Forbes-Bosely's word that was taken as the truth. I was to learn quite early however that Thomas Forbes-Bosely's word was not to be trusted!

We first met when we were both assigned to carry out a raid on a village where we arrested several bad hats who were suspected of being thugs. They were put in irons and taken away to be questioned, and eventually they were to be tried.

"Waste of time", said Forbes-Bosely.

"We should hang 'em now. It would teach all the others that we mean business. I suppose though that you namby-pamby lot want to convert them. Waste of time."

I tried to stay calm in the face of this provocation, but I really lost my temper when Forbes-Bosely put his spurs to his pony and rode through one of the huts smashing what little possessions the poor Indian woman had left to her who had just seen her husband arrested and taken away. She sat amidst the ruins of her home cradling a broken teraphim.

"Was that really necessary?"

Forbes-Bosely looked at me in feigned amazement.

"I do beg your pardon", he said sardonically.

"Was it really necessary to destroy those few poor belongings of that wretched woman?"

Here I must own that I allowed my voice to be raised which seemed to amuse Forbes-Bosely immensely. I realised later when I overheard him telling someone that he had "got my goat" that he was deliberately baiting me, hoping that I might strike him, and to be honest I have to admit that at that moment I could have willingly struck him. As he went on I felt my face redden. He was a bounder, a cad.

"Driscoll, She's the wife of a thug."

"You don't know that. Anyway that's no excuse for smashing

her meagre things, surely to God!"

"What are you Driscoll? Some sort of nigger lover? Aha! now I have it. You thought you could have her, and I've spoilt it for you. "I'm so sorry old chap. You should have said."

Now I really lost my temper. His mock humility on top of his wicked slur on my honourable conduct incensed me. I pulled my pony up short and turned towards him.

"You unspeakable..." I began, but was interrupted when one of the bearers called out:

"Lord. Look, there's a fire."

We cantered back to find the hut that Forbes-Bosely had smashed his way through was well alight. Had the woman set light to it in despair at losing everything? Or was Forbes-Bosely's actions responsible for overturning a cooking pot or lotah that spilled ghee onto the fire and so caused the conflagration? It was never fully determined. What was sure however was that Forbes-Bosely did not care one jot.

From that time on I tried to avoid Forbes-Bosely, but he remained an aggravating thorn in my flesh on more than one occasion. What finally brought matters to a head was the Padma Sivalatti affair. We got word that another case of Chandee Pooja had taken place. What's more we were given specific details about it so we were able to go there straightaway. Raj Dal and Mamoud Patel had brought around the ponies anticipating that I would not wish to lose this opportunity to take swift action, and we lost no time in setting off, not even stopping for a meal. Raj Dal put some chapattis in a saddlebag along with some wine. I hoped to catch the perpetrators of this dastardly act, but Raj Dal warned me however that we would most certainly be too late for that. A look at my Waterbury convinced me that he was probably correct.

Getting the place where we had been told the men and girl had been seen, we went into a mullah, forcing our way through the thorny scrub, ever watchful as I suspected a trap. The heat was intense for it was during the hottest part of the day when sensible sahibs were resting on their beds and even natives were on their charpoys in whatever shade they could find. I felt the sweat run down my thighs as I gripped my pony's fat belly, anxious not to be swept off by any vegetation. Raj Dal called out:

"There she is."

We spurred our ponies forward to see a young girl nearby a Dhak tree who was embedded in the ground ahead of us. Her kohl encrusted eyes looked at us impassively. I turned to Raj Dal who said before I could ask:

"Drugged"

She was covered in finery, all intended to make her into a miniscule version of the goddess. I had heard of this practice of Chandee Pooja but had never, until this moment, seen it. Up to this minute, to be truthful, I had always doubted such tales, dismissing them as traveller's tales that had been exaggerated for a greater effect upon credulous listeners. Now in the heat with the flies buzzing around us I had living proof before me. It was living proof because we had acted quickly and she was still alive. Had she been left out the day before, God alone knows what her fate might have been. I had seen young goats tethered as bait for tigers and the way that they had been left out came to my mind. In those cases however, the guns were waiting for the tiger and the kid was often saved.

We dismounted and a syce held the reins of our nervous ponies. It was an easy job to dig her out. She obeyed Raj Dal with a total lack of emotion as he got her to lift one leg and then the other until she was free. The syce muttered something in a dialect that I did not understand. Raj Dal turned on him furiously and replied in the same dialect as far as I could follow it. Whatever it was, it made the syce look very frightened.

"He says that we will offend the goddess. He also says that her parents will not wish her to be returned to them as she belongs now to the goddess, so why are we doing this?"

I must own that I felt utter amazement. Despite having seen many strange things since coming to this strange land, this must surely be the strangest!

"Her parents will not take her back?"

"No sahib. She has been given to the goddess. She belongs to her."

"But what would have happened to if we had not rescued her?"

By now we were returning and Raj Dal had her sitting in front of him on his pony. He shrugged

"No food. No water. What do you think? She might survive a night, but a wild animal would probably get her eventually."

I was appalled,at the girl's possible fate, but more appalled at Raj Dal's seeming indifference. Later I came to realise that he was not unsympathetic, but realistic. He was simply accepting the status quo. In my position with John Company I could not however, and luckily I had a solution to the problem of what to do with little Padma Sivalatti who by now was coming out of the trance that had been induced by the drugs that had been given her.

I accepted Raj Dal's situation. After all I was only a firenghi and some things you could change and others not. In fact it could be very dangerous to meddle without being sure about all the facts. Look at that time when we tried to rescue a young woman from her husband's funeral pyre. She was to be suttee. It was illegal but still went on. We got her away only to find that she ran back and voluntarily immolated herself, and to add to our troubles, her relatives made death threats not against me, but against my servants, some of whom deserted me in fright.

Without knowing that there was a place immediately available in the Queen Victoria Home for Girls that had recently been opened, I had her taken to my bungalow; this was a mistake, but luckily before I went home she had already been moved to the Home. The following day I was called into the main office where I was told that Sir George Fielding wished to see me. Full of myself for having carried out what I considered to be a clever rescue, I went in only to find myself interrogated as if I had committed an offence!

"What's this I hear about you taking a little girl away from her parents without their consent?"

Standing behind him was Forbes-Bosely grinning at me as I tried to to explain why I had done what I had done. He cut me short, saying:

"Fond of little girl's are you?"

Forbes-Bosely's grin became even wider. He winked at me from behind Sir George's back.

Chapter 4

1838

'
Tis all a Chequer-board of Nights and Days
Where Destiny with Men for Pieces plays:
Hither and thither moves, and mates, and slays,
And one by one back in the Closet lays.

I felt sick as I looked as Forbes-Bosely's grin and saw him wink. The wink told me that I had been trapped by my good nature and his evil design upon me to do me a real mischief. He then made the mistake of allowing himself to laugh. Sir George Fielding whirled around and said furiously:

"Get out you insolent young pup. This is no subject for humour."

Forbes-Bosely's grin changed to a smile of indifference. Taking up his hat he sauntered out and I think that it was his attitude that made Sir George Fielding question me more closely about the Padma Sivalatti affair and how I had come to be involved. My explanation was accepted and I was pleased to note that it was recorded along with some adverse remarks that I made about Forbes-Bosely's conduct. I waited until the note was finished listening to the steady creaking of the punkah above our heads. The windows had been covered with woven grass screens that were regularly splashed with water to try to keep the rooms cool. Instead the water as it evaporated made the atmosphere even more humid.

Despite the damp heat I sat there waiting for I was certain that Sir George Fielding had not finished with me. He looked up at me with those washed out blue eyes of his and filled his pipe slowly; he eschewed cigars. When it was lit and was emitting the usual pungent smell he spoke at last.

"So what are we to do with you now? It might be sensible if we were to put you somewhere other than here for a spell."

He paused and pretended to think. I say pretended for he was a wily old bird and I was sure that he had already decided my fate. I was sure that I was to be banished to some outlandish spot that I had never heard of where I would never be heard of either. He tamped the bowl of his pipe and said mildly.

"Good with languages ain't you?"

I sat up straighter. This sounded more promising.

Yes sir, Urdu, Pushtu some Gujerati..."

"...Yes, yes, yes. I know all that. Well there's an..."

He hesitated.

"There's an expedition that's going to Kabul. You do know where Kabul is I take it."

I nodded. I was excited. Everybody had heard of this 'expedition' that was a thinly disguised attempt to take over Afghanistan and stick another ruler on the throne who would be more sympathetic to British interests.

"Right. Well here's a chitty that you can take over to the commissariat where they will kit you out and give you all the details that you need to go along with the main force. Now listen to me carefully. You are not part of the fighting force. You are on attachment only to give such assistance as you can by using your knowledge of the language and customs of these benighted heathens. Oh! and one more thing. Whatever you hear, whatever you understand, it would be useful for the department to know about. I expect you will find a way to pass on any such details so that they do not become common knowledge. I might tell you that your finding such a way and the quality of what you send to us will very much influence your future."

I left the office in a state of extreme jubilation. Outside I found Forbes-Bosely lolling against the wall smoking a cheroot. Immediately I was alert and on my guard. I tried to look hangdog.

"Sorry old chap", he offered, " I had to keep old Fielders informed y'know. So what's to become of you?"

"I'm to be sent away. That's what is to become of me. Now if you will excuse me I must pack."

He tried to keep the gloating out of his voice.

"Oh! bad luck old chap. Somewhere nasty I expect."

I said nothing. He would hear soon enough. Gossip went round faster than cholera most times. I pushed past him and he reluctantly moved back to let me pass. Later I heard that Sir George Fielding had heard this exchange and had commented that I seemed to have grasped what I was supposed to be about!

I was told to choose only one servant to go with me and that man Raj Dal. I had already found him infinitely ready to serve me in all respects so I told him that he would be my bearer during the time that I was away from my bungalow. I could not have chosen a better man. Later on in my career I also had Mamoud Patel who accompanied me wherever I went. I completely trusted these two men and had good reason to as you will see.

Raj Dal seemed to know all the gossip and as he packed for me he told me about Dost Muhammad who was Afghanistan's Emir.

"It is said everywhere Sahib that Dost Muhammad wants to be the great friend of the British but wishes us to attack his enemies first."

"Who are...?"

Raj Dal spread his hands to indicate apparent ignorance but then went on:

"Whoever they are, they hold Peshawar, and the Emir wants it back."

I remembered having read that the Sikhs had captured Peshawar in 1834 just before I came out to India. Raj Dal must have known this and had pleaded ignorance of this fact as he wished to give me a diplomatic answer. I was pleased to hear this as I thought it showed tact. Later on I found Raj Dal was inclined to tell me what he thought I wanted to hear, 'though as we got to know each other better he told me honestly what he thought. He now added that when we said 'no' to such an attack Dost Muhammad had started to talk to the Russians.

"They mean no good to anyone, those Russians. I hear that they are not even proper Christians like your honour."

So that was what all this was about. Lord Auckland had probably thought that as a result of all the discussions that he had had that Dost Muhammad was anti-British. I thought that he was wrong. I was of the opinion that Dost Muhammad was just playing off one strong power against another to see which one might best serve his interests. It had become rather urgent recently though for Russia had set up an army along with the Persians and seemed intent on overrunning Afghanistan, having abandoned any idea of trying to make a treaty with the Emir.

Lord Auckland as Governor General of India had immense power. So, as he was actually in India, his plan to drive away the Russians and the Persians and install a ruler in Afghanistan who was pro-British was accepted in Britain. Personally I thought better the devil you know... Anyway, Lord Auckland chose Shuja Shah Durrani to be in charge of Afghanistan instead of Dost Muhammad. It made a certain amount of sense for Shuja Shah Durrani was, after all, the former ruler of Afghanistan. I never really understood why he had been deposed and was living in exile in Lahore. I took the trouble to read about him and although I still could not see why he had been deposed I found out that he had been on our side during the Napoleonic Wars against Russia and France, having formed useful positive alliances. So there you are. Do not, I beg you, worry too much about the names; the main thing to remember was that I was involved.

No one seemed sorry to see me depart except Joan Biddlesworth. I said goodbye to her and she said that she would miss our conversations. I thought that she probably would, for she must have been bored to the point of screaming just to relieve the monotony of her daily round. I must have been the only bright part of her life at that time. Then the whole thing very nearly got called off. We had three divisions all ready to sail and march, but before we could start we heard that the Persian and the Russian army had abandoned the siege of Herat. Any sensible diplomat would have gone back to sweet-talking Dost Muhammad. I heard a lot of officers say just this. I must say here that it is often from the middle ranking officers that you hear the most sense. The young ones don't know enough, and the older ones are either too far removed from the dust bowl of action or too ready to suck up to the top dogs. But Lord Auckland was not to be swayed. He simply decided that we should go ahead with his plan. Part of our forces were now to be left behind in reserve, and I very nearly got left behind with them, but somewhat mysteriously I was included in the force that was to march to Kabul.

Yes, I know what you are going to say, and you are right. I did no marching. My progress was on a horse. Raj Dal managed to find a pony so he avoided the tramping that was done by most of the army; and many of them were barefoot. They had been all their lives so it was no real hardship for them until we got much higher and it got much colder. Naturally I also had several other servants. It might be of interest to list them here for I know from conversations that I have had back in England people are woefully ignorant of what goes on in India.

The person that I have already mentioned was my personal servant. In addition I also had someone to care for my horse. Naturally I needed someone to prepare my food and someone to put up my tent and take it down; and, as it had to be carried, along with a native bed for me to sleep on, I needed a bullock cart. Of course the bullock cart needed a driver, and so it went on. At least I was not at that time married so I did not require a palaquin for my good lady. Lots of others did, so you can imagine what our whole assembly resembled. Yes that's see some it exactly - a rabble! As we moved along I was reminded of Exodus, for surely the Israelites as they left Egypt led by Moses and Aaron must have looked just as we did.

And maybe sounded and smelled as we did as well; for what with horses neighing, bullocks lowing and goats bleating, not to mention the shouting in several languages as everyone tried to be part of this vast conclave as it moved so slowly along what was luckily a dusty road, I can only describe it as a permanent uproar. India always smelled, some would say stank. But it was of a different order to the foul smell that one suffered in London. There, the streets were filthy and as a result the filth emitted a constant disgusting effluvium. Here, somehow the overall smell seemed more exotic, mingled as it was with spices and sandal wood and the smell of chapattis being cooked. I expect my memory is probably deficient and were I to go back now I would be appalled at the stench, so unlike what I now enjoy in leafy Surbiton with its well swept streets.

But, just now and again as I walk those streets I imagine the street scene in India with its elephants dressed like Indian brides, carefully putting down one enormous foot after another sending up puffs of ochre dust at each step, camels linked together in long loose padding chains and flocks of goats driven by urchins whose clothing is never more than scraps of coloured rags, and I wish I could be there once more.

Our quickest way would have been through the Punjab and up the Khyber Pass. I am sure that you will have heard of that. No? Oh the youth of today, what do they teach you? That route was denied to us by Ranjit Singh, the ruler of the Punjab, who still had enough clout to say no to Lord Auckland.   So the Governor General of India's army didn't have the luxury of crossing the Punjab. You can see how it was in those days. Lord Auckland might be styled Governor General of India, but his power and authority were not absolute, so we had to take another route; this one was much longer and went through the southern passes.

Our journey seemed to take forever. That did not bother me. I was young and the young think that they have all the time in the world, but eventually we reached Kandahar, which simply just surrendered! I was disappointed. Although not officially a combatant I had hoped to see something more than the seemingly endless marching and pitching camp and striking it again. However, encouraged by this, and despite having lost many troops and horses due to sheer incompetence, our generals pushed on to Ghazni. Now this Ghazni had a fort and it was one that we had to take if we were to reach our objective. I looked at it and I thought this was not going to be so easy.

Nor would it have been had it not been for a traitor to Hyder Khan, the son of Dost Muhammad who was leading the defence of the fort. We later put it about that we obtained some information from some captured soldiers about a considerably less well-defended gateway. Actually Raj Dal told me afterwards that we had paid a large sum of rupees to someone inside the fort to ensure that the gate was sufficiently sabotaged so that when our sappers went in and put explosives against it, it caved in easily. I learned a valuable lesson that day: money well spent can save time and lives; you might have to be a bit unethical of course.

Despite paying out our rupees we still did not have any other option than a frontal assault, for we had lost so much of our provisions and horses and siege weapons by going round the long way that this frontal attack was our only chance. Anyway it worked for as I said we were attacking a deliberately weakened gate and several people got medals and honours as a result. Not me, of course. I was well to the rear and making sure that everything I heard and saw was written down and sent back. Would you believe that I used the device of sending back my dirty laundry with notes hidden inside? Everyone who heard that I was so pernickety that I had to send my shirts back and that I also demanded clean underwear be sent to me, thought that I was barking mad. That was how I began to get a reputation for quirkiness, a reputation that I used several times. I was also known as the sahib who always needed a chutter to keep off the sun as much as the rain for I tended to go red with too much sun.

After Ghazni it was plain sailing to press on to Kabul. Luckily Ghazni Fort was so well provisioned that by taking it we managed to march on without having to wait for supplies to be sent up. In no time at all we had got rid of Dost Muhammad and replaced him with Shuja Shah Durrani. I had read 'The Prince ' by Machiavelli and thought that we should have gone after Dost Muhammad and got rid of him permanently. We didn't, so when I was sent back from Kabul to India in 1840 with the bulk of the troops I thought that there was going to be trouble especially as there were so many civilians left there in Kabul along with our troops. Civilians are always trouble.

Afghanistan is a large country. It is not inhabited by Afghanistans as such. It is occupied by tribes who form allegiances with each other until they think it better to go back on their word and form other alliances. You certainly cannot control the whole country from one town. Nor should you think that because one tribe supports you for the moment that you are safely in control. You ain't, and never will be. Afghanistan is not Wales. But stupidly that's what McNaughten tried to do. And, just as I predicted Dost Muhammad started to make trouble. But even I was appalled at how we were to be driven out of Afghanistan.

By the way, I realise that I am taking a while to get to the nub of my story, but I think that it is necessary to provide all these details to explain how I got involved. Bear with me then chaps. I say chaps, as I cannot believe women would be the slightest bit interested in my tale, bless their hearts!

Actually, I now have to retract that statement, for I need to tell you here about Fanny Parkes whom I met and immediately liked enormously. Please do understand that our friendship was just that – friendship. She was married but used her husband's position to move around freely. In point of fact Fanny made friends with everyone and anyone as her book tells in great detail. I do not suppose anyone reads it now. She was interested in everything and made a fetish of writing down what she saw and heard to such an extent that she quite upset some of the other memsahibs who thought that her behaviour was letting down her sex. I found her to be quite refreshing. Now that I have set this down I am beginning to think that Fanny used me, just as she used everyone, by her sheer force of personality; she was excitement personified, so she dragged along everyone in her wake, me included!

She never actually said that she even liked me, but the occasional hand laid on my sleeve as she explained some obscure bit of Hindoo   mythology led me to believe that her interest in me was more than a passing one. I imagined that I sensed that were she to be free from her marital state her readiness to spend time in my company meant something other than mere friendship. Could I have been mistaken? There is only one answer to that question: men's capacity for self-deception is unlimited.

One of my abiding memories is when we both went to see Kumbh Mela. This only occurs every twelve years. It is an extremely holy event and one that I thought Fanny ought never to have gone to see. I was used to the nudity of the men and their extreme behaviour, but I thought that she might be shocked at the complete lack of inhibition that was a feature of this mass ritual bathing in the Ganges. When I put this to her she merely laughed at me and reminded me how together we had witnessed the hook-swinging.

It was true that I had gone with her on that occasion and sat in the hot dust beside her as above us a hooked swinger revolved in the humid night and showered us and other onlookers with garlands and sweetmeats. She had shown an unusual interest in watching as two iron hooks had been inserted into the native's bare back. She even stood up to see how the hooks were pushed below the shoulder blades and then tied together with a rope. As he was then hauled up to be suspended from a wooden apparatus that consisted of an upright pole and a horizontal cross beam her mouth opened in excitement. I'm afraid that it bored me. She, on the other hand, seemed to be energised by it. The fact that the native endured all the pain with stoicism appeared to disappoint her. I do not know quite what she hoped to get from witnessing charak puja; she said afterwards that she wanted to see everything that India had to show her.

I told her that self-torture plays an important role in the cult of Shiva and that she could see an abundance of similar actions during Samnyasa. Ascetics, sannyas, perform all manner of ascetic exercises during this time such as piercing their tongues, walking on knives and generally abusing their bodies in a variety of ways, not unlike some Christian saints I suppose, like that one who lived on a pillar for most of his life.

Eventually I gave in and we went to Allahabad to see the Kumbh Mela, but I made her wear native dress as I thought that otherwise she would stand out and attract too much attention. Thinking about that time now when we wandered together among the sadhus, some of whom were clad in saffron sheets with ashes and colours dabbed on their skin, and others who wore nothing at all, I wonder if I was wise to indulge her. If I had not been so ready to go along with her would she not have been more restrained? But I remember how we were nearly bowled over when a trident wielding naked group of holy men charged together to reach the sacred Ganges at what they considered to be a propitious moment to embrace Mother Ganges, and she screamed not from fear, but from pleasure; I'm of the opinion that Fanny was already well out of hand!

Naturally I called upon Joan Biddlesworth when I returned, more out of a sense of duty really. The poor girl had nothing to occupy her days so I thought that the least I could do was offer her some conversation.

I was not at all pleased however to be verbally chastised by her for preferring a married lady's company to hers! It seemed that she had somehow got it into her head that my calling on her meant more than my carrying out a simple Christian duty; she appeared to think that I had other interests in her!

Chapter 5

1840-1850

Beware the snake who lurks beneath
the shining trembling tender leaf
But better still beware the hand
that seeks to rob you of your land

Safely back from Kabul and installed snugly in the Thuggee and Dacoitry Department I settled into a routine that was all the more pleasant as during my time away my arch enemy, Forbes-Bosely, had been posted elsewhere. Rumour had it that this had been occasioned by an affair that he had had with a married woman. He was posted and she died of cholera. At least that was the story put about, but Mamoud Patel was able to tell me that she had died following a botched attempt to deal with an unwanted pregnancy.

I did not ask where he had got this story, nor did I rebuke him as I perhaps should have for his disloyalty to the white men who were now so rightly in charge of his country. Instead I murmured something to the effect that some people were cads and their behaviour confirmed this fact of life if they were given enough opportunity to demonstrate this fact. One officer who was certainly not a cad was Albert Hervey.

When I met Albert Hervey I was pleased to see that he was exactly the opposite of Forbes-Bosely. He had come to India as I had after going through the rigours of Addiscombe so we had quite a great deal in common. We had many a laugh together at some of the exploits that he said he was going to put into a book that he was writing. I wondered whether they were all true but he assured me that they were. He then went

47

on to tell me that he was going to put the whole truth in even if it embarrassed those that he exposed.

I asked him whether it was the wisest course of action to write in his proposed book such criticisms as he expounded to me? I told him that while I admired his adherence to the truth, might it not be more politic to temper the truth with a modicum of caution? His reply of 'fiddlesticks' told me that he was bent on a course of action that I could only perceive as one that would lead to disaster for him if he wished to continue a career in the military in India. Despite my forebodings I still thought that Albert was a really decent cove. We drank to that in ice-cold claret which went down particularly well in the sweltering heat. Then we repaired to our separate residences to sleep away the afternoon. Well, I did, but Albert went out hunting as usual and bagged several snipe, which feat of arms earned him some respect and also some gratitude for it increased our larder to everyone's satisfaction.

Everyone was sorry when Albert got married and returned to England. He was a thoroughly nice chap and a good shot. In due course his book appeared and I took the trouble to send for a copy and read it. I was gratified to see that several people who were named in it only appeared as initials, so my advice was taken. I think that one of the situations described by him might have been about me, but I am not saying which one! I looked for my copy of his book the other day, but like so many things that I had in India it had suffered from the onslaught of the climate and insects and was no more.

It was just after this time that I met Fanny Parkes again. I can quite understand how Fanny had succumbed to the spell of India becoming more and more Indian in her clothing and attitudes, much to the annoyance of some of her contemporaries. From time to time when our paths crossed as she moved around India I marvelled at the increasing change that I observed in her. I was amused 'tho when her book was published in 1850, and I shall say more about this later. In the meantime I must return to my account for I am sure that you will be wanting to know about my progress rather than chat about characters like Fanny or Joan Biddlesworth.

Before I go on about my progress I ought to mention here that when we heard that Arthur Connolly had been captured while trying to rescue one of our chaps no one seriously considered that he nor the chap he was trying to rescue was in any real danger. How wrong we were! They were both charged with being spies and put to death. They were actually beheaded in public; a great disgrace for us to have to endure. But there was worse to come.

Throughout our connection with India we have always been suspicious that Russia would try to move in somehow and supplant us. India has always provided us with great wealth, and we have always been determined to maintain that flow of wealth. We did not want Russia to take that away from us. You only have to look at Clive of India who did so much for   the East India Company. I know he was a superb soldier, but he was also one for the booty; and because he secured so much for the Company they were happy to see him go home with so much wealth that everyone was jealous of it. I imagine that you have been told that the way in which he shook the pagoda tree was not available to later personages such as myself; but be not mistaken. Excess wealth may not have been available but quite adequate sums were.

But if we were to continue to draw on his wealth it meant that we had constantly to show the Russians that we were prepared to take firm action; that was why we had gone into Kabul. So it was with extra horror that I heard that so many perished when in 1842 we were driven out of Afghanistan. The extra horror was the fact that behind such a disaster must be the hand of Russia. Someone had obviously helped the Afghanistans who are basically just a series of tribesmen, very brave, of course, but normally totally disorganised. It must have been the Russians. I am sure they were behind this in providing the organisation that was necessary. It was proved to my satisfaction in due course by the easy way in which we sent an army of retribution back into Afghanistan. By then the game was up and the Russians, fearing that if their participation behind the scenes were to become too public we might move against them, quickly faded away out of sight. In fact it all became quiet for some time.

I was also persuaded that my reading of events was the correct one when I met Sir Henry Creswicke Rawlinson in London in 1851 as I shall relate in my next chapter. I was also to meet Fanny Parkes again as I made it my business to seek her out when I came to England on leave hoping to renew our acquaintance and to chew over our experiences. I think that as this account is very unlikely to be published I can admit here that I secretly hoped for more from such a meeting than an interesting discussion.

In the meantime I almost took part in what was considered to be one of the most, or possibly the most, successful battle to have ever taken place in India. This was in January 1846. I have since seen it written that it was: 'a battle without a mistake'. Now I am not going to make the mistake of telling you all about it here. I shall leave it to the historians. All I need to say is that I was part of the army commanded by Sir Hugh Gough, the then Governor-General of Bengal. I have to admit that we were first of all driven back by the Sikhs who did terrible slaughter our troops. Luckily we were not attacked again so were able to rest somewhat. But when they did so we had a hero in the making: this was Sir Harry Smith who was sent to assist us. He cleverly force-marched his troops and then completely routed the enemy. I won't go into details; you can read all about it in the history books. Sir Harry Smith said afterwards:

'I have gained one of the most glorious battles ever fought in India.'

You might consider that he was being a little presumptuous and might have left such a comment to others, but the point I wish to make here is that later in my career I was to fetch up in Ladysmith in South Africa; yes, the Ladysmith town that was relieved and sent all London into wild rejoicing. I expect you know all about that episode in London, might even have been there? No? Well never mind, what you might not know is that Ladysmith was named as such by Sir Harry Smith after his good lady wife.

Chapter 6

1851-1854

Shaitan's influence is everywhere to be seen and felt.

It was cool enough to travel with some pleasure through the countryside even though the place I was sent to was not that pleasurable for the prisoners. It was Agra prison, the main prison that we used for those thuggee assailants who we managed to find guilty. No, they were not all hanged. Sometimes the evidence was not sufficiently clear to do this. We locked them up instead. In the past several of them had tried to escape, even cutting through the bars of their cells by coating a few of their long hairs with oil and corborundum powder to do so. As a result I was told a policy of keeping the prisoners totally employed at all time was introduced as a means to avoid similar attempts. It seemed a good idea to me.

"Satan finds work for idle hands", I said.

"Indeed, Shaitan's influence is everywhere to be seen and felt", replied the overseer, an ex Subadar who was well known to me.

He led me now to a hot low-roofed workshop where I saw the prisoners working on a great carpet. It was nearly finished and I had been chose to accompany it to England where it was to be exhibited at the Great Exhibition. I was due to have some leave so the authorities had decided to kill two birds with the stone of my trip home. Joan Biddlesworth said that she quite envied me in getting not only to see England but also the queen and the exhibition. She was, of course, still unwed and now exhibited a certain waspishness in her tone of voice. I readily forgave her. Her situation was one that would have appalled me had I to endure it. She made me promise that I would call on her on my return when she wished to hear everything about my trip.

The carpet was superb and I must admit that the prisoners who had worked upon it and knew that it was destined to be seen by the Queen were most enthusiastic. I had expected them to be lethargic about this aspect of their work, but found them to be not only proud of their efforts (as they had every right to be for it was a superb example of native workmanship) but also delighted that it was to be seen by their queen.

My trip home was much more luxurious than my first trip out had been, I can tell you. Having charge of the carpet gave me a cachet that I exploited to the full. And why not pray? Getting the damned thing to the exhibition was a nightmare that made me sweat more from anxiety than I ever did from the sun in Rajisthan. I still wake from dreams about that woven square where I am convinced that it is either on fire or has been dropped off the side of the boat or some other nameless mishap has occurred to it.

As I prepared myself for the Great Exhibition in my hotel room in London I looked into the mirror and was not displeased with what I saw there. The man who looked back at me did not look thirty-two; he still had most of his hair, which I must admit was a little less fiery than it had been, and his whiskers would not have disgraced the finest cavalry officer. I smiled showing that I still had most of my teeth, although I have to admit that I had to be careful on which side I chewed my meat. I brushed up my whiskers, pulled in my stomach, did up my belt, and buckled on my sword for I was to be presented to Her Majesty the Queen. Behind me I heard what I can only be described as a snigger. Standing by the door was the maid who had brought up my hot water. It comes to something when men such as I are laughed at by mere maids. But, as I might have mentioned before, I am not at all vain, so I was able ignore her pert behaviour.

I took up my place alongside the carpet that had caused me so many sleepless nights. It struck me at the last minute as the royal party approached that perhaps the maid may have been amused at something that she had seen that I could not have spied in the mirror. 'Too late', I thought preparing to bow wondering whether I had somehow left a shirt-tail hanging out. I need not have worried. No one of any note looked at me. There were too many more important personages present than I to be goggled at.

At least Her Majesty looked at the carpet, but just when I was to be presented to her, the Duke of Wellington arrived and I was elbowed aside. I was still close enough to hear the conversation however. Waving a pale pudgy be-ringed little hand at the sparrows that were fouling the exhibits, she asked the Iron Duke what might be done about them. She had removed her gloves for the heat inside what was essentially a vast hot house was intense. Her overdressed Ladies in Waiting looked quite pale. His laconic answer has stayed forever fresh in my memory:

"Sparrow Hawks Ma-am."

There was a general laugh and a smile from the queen and they all moved on. I was left to brush off the bird droppings from the carpet. I then abandoned it, deeming that I had more than fulfilled my duty and went off to enjoy my leave. In time I heard that the carpet fetched up in a room in Windsor Castle so someone must have liked it; it might even have been Queen Victoria herself. My mind however was full of how I had arranged to meet Fanny Parkes so the final destiny of the carpet was of much less importance to me at that moment.

It was my knowledge of what Fanny had written in her book that got me leave to call upon her. In the meantime I was briefly to meet a Captain Louis Edward Nolan who had also come from India on leave. We were both at a levee where I recognised his uniform and introduced myself as another man on leave from India. He spent most of his time with me asking me about horses and their schooling, an area of life in India of which I had really only very limited experience. I heard much later that he considered himself somewhat of an authority on how to train horses for their use as cavalry mounts and was writing a book on the subject. It would not have surprised me to find that his conversation with me was to pick my brains for what I might know about horses. He left me to pay his respects to Lady Elstree and it was not very pleasant to hear him say as he spoke to her something that sounded like:

"Quite a stupid chap really, no ideas..."

Of course he could have been alluding to someone else, but as his eyes were on me at the time I have no doubt that I was the person under discussion. I turned away feeling a certain chagrin, for although I was ready to dismiss him from my thoughts, what he had said still rankled.

"Do not distress yourself", said somebody who had seen my encounter and had also been privy to the subsequent snatch of conversation that I had overheard. He went on:

56

"We have never met, but I have seen something of your work."

He introduced himself. I knew of him of course. How could anyone employed in the British East India Company not know him? Although he was first and foremost an army officer, I knew that he had a worldwide reputation as an Orientalist, mainly because of his knowledge of Assyriology. He was in London now to publish some important work before going out to do more digging. 'Oh dear', I thought, for if I knew little about training horses I certainly knew far less about the Assyrians.

He suggested that we might retire from the levee and go to his club for a quiet drink. I agreed immediately and was soon rattling along on a cab while he began to tell me something of his political beliefs. Now I was as astounded as I expect you are to hear that Sir Henry Creswicke Rawlinson had taken it on himself to do this. All became clearer however when we were settled in the smoking room of his club in Pall Mall.

I knew that he was one of the foremost figures around who advocated the stopping of any Russian activity in South Asia. This was not an approach shared by all of course. Apparently he had read my reports that I had sent back as I went to Kabul. He shared my opinion that all the events in Afghanistan were set off by the Russians.

" I like the way you include even the most trivial details", he told me.

My cheeks flamed, and not just because of the brandy and soda that a club servant had brought us.

"I expect that you know that I think that we should retain Kandahar. We need a presence there. I am sure that Russia is going to attack and take into their empire such places as Khokand. In time they will do the same with Bokhara and Khiva. We have to show that we are strong."

It now became clear as to why I had been singled out. Sir Henry was going to be engaged in his work in what was Assyria. While he was there he would be kept in touch with what was happening in India because he would still be an officer in the East India Company. He would be sent copies of official documents etc. What he wanted from me however was a less formal, but more detailed account of anything that pertained to Russia's interests that I might come across. His parting remark to me was:

"Remember, it's the apparently trivial detail that interests me. No matter how insignificant you might consider it to be, I shall read it assiduously."

I shall not bore you with the details of how I was to fulfil my task. It's sufficient to say that I was approached by someone anonymously who explained everything to me that I was to do in the finest detail.

Filled with a new sense of my importance in the great scheme of things and suitably bolstered in my self-esteem I sought out and visited Fanny Parkes who you will remember I knew in India. She had returned to England and had published a book about her wanderings in India. She was now living in Marylebone and when I called I first made sure that I spoke first with her husband, Major Zachariah Parkes, who initially eyed me suspiciously with slightly blood-shot eyes until I explained who I was. Once he knew that I was part of John Company everything changed and his suspicions fell away. He told me that he thought that I was one of those damned journalistic fellas; for apparently ever since his wife had written that book they had swarmed about her like blasted flies round a dead pi dog. Of course we had a peg or two togeher. I would have been satisfied with a chota peg, but nothing would suit him unless we 'drank like men'.

He had a thriving architectural and surveyors practice, having overcome his first horror of actually being in business. In fact I was told by someone who had had dealings with the firm that most of the work was done by qualified underlings; juniors who did the skilled work while he sweet-talked the clientele.

After a while Fanny joined us. What a change! This was not the dear sweet Fanny that I remembered all dressed in flowing robes looking so colourful and lively. I recalled that someone recently had described her as an old crow now rather than a bird of paradise. Of course this was partly because she was in mourning. However I saw now immediately what they meant. Gone was the lively humorous bright, intellectually bright that is, woman. Now I was speaking instead to a woman who seemed to have returned to what must have seemed to her to be a form of imprisonment. I could see that she was not only clad in stays, if you will forgive me the impropriety of mentioning such a garment, but hemmed in and around with the whole panoply of social customs that kept her in thrall. She had escaped to India only to return to captivity.

In her usual clear- sighted way she described to me her disappointment on returning to England where she had anticipated pretty May flowers and spring sunshine upon her arrival. Alas! Her memories of England in the spring were as false as my memories will be of India. There was for her instead a welcome of cold rain mixed with sleet, and bitter winds that brought the wet sleet into her face like a savage attack on one who had dared to forsake her native country. Actually, if you go far enough north in India the climate and weather can be similar to that awful country Wales! Even the houses depressed her, she said, as they were built of cold grey slate and gloomy stone.

To cheer her up I talked about India and as we did so she gradually became more animated. I congratulated her on her book. We lamented that so few in England seemed to be concerned with India and all its many facets. She had, of course gone to India well before I went there and her book was a marvel of its time insofar as it recorded so accurately so much that everyone simply took for granted then. In so doing she provided future generations with a picture of an India that has long since departed for India has changed dramatically. When she was there we moved around on horseback or bullock wagons, or palaquins for the ladies. This was still the case to a certain degree, but it was changing, and would alter even more when railways that were presently being constructed in Europe began to be built across India's enormous hinterland.

As our conversation continued I sensed that her interest in me no longer existed, if it ever did. I was just a welcome diversion in what was now a humdrum life. I think that I had fooled myself in even considering that she might have seen in me a possible... I think perhaps that I had better stop here before I reveal how immense had been my self-deception. Instead I will confess how my frustration following our conversation led me into temptation.

I had returned to the hotel where I saw that chit of a girl, that pert maid had giggled at the sight of me as I had readied myself to meet my queen. I was climbing the stairs to go to my room and would have passed her without a glance had she not plucked at my sleeve in the most intimate manner. I stopped and looked at her severely. I was about to say something for her behaviour deserved a rebuke. I turned towards her. She really was an appealing young woman I noted, despite her forwardness. I hardened my heart as she said:

"Oh sir, can you forgive me? I did not know that your honour was such an important person and that your uniform was necessary as you were to meet the queen. I should not have laughed at you, I really should not have."

My heart was touched. My sympathy was aroused. Here was someone who recognised what I represented, probably a country girl having to make her way in London by herself. I decided to be magnanimous. I smiled at her.

Seeing that I was not going to chide her, as I should have done, she went on:

"You are probably one of those heroes, what the vicar back home calls 'unsung'. He tells me to be brave and keep cheerful, but it ain't easy I can tell you when you ain't got your beau to hand."

"Where is he?"

He's in India, a soldier. I ain't heard nothing from him for so long."

Tears were now sliding down her red cheeks. I wiped them away clumsily as this was not something that I normally found myself doing. Encouraged by this she pressed herself to me and whispered:

"Oh sir. You are such a comfort to me."

She then kissed me, and I have to admit that I then quite lost my head for I led her into my room to offer her more comfort of a like nature where she eventually allowed me the utmost liberties. I need not dwell upon what these were. For if you have ever been in my position I have no doubt that if you fell too, as I did, led astray by lies, then you will already know what these liberties were that this minx allowed me; and if you have never been led astray in this fashion then I think it better not to tamper with your innocence.

Yes, I know I should have been strong and resisted temptation, but it was the old story; the one where a virtuous man is led astray by a wicked woman. For when I had finished she demanded money from me, saying that it was difficult for an honest country girl as she was to make a living in London. As if that were not enough she then complained that the amount that I finally pressed into her hand to be rid of her was scarcely sufficient, adding to my chagrin, that the competition was so severe!

If any thing else encouraged me to go back to India immediately this episode certainly did. I still had some furlough owing to me, but I decided that London was no place for me. In any case my finances were low; that young woman had taken the last of what I had set aside to see the sights. The art galleries would have to wait for me, as would the music halls. I have to allow that I think that I regretted not seeing more of the latter than the former.

Chapter 7

1851-1854

"How sweet is mortal Sovranty!"---think some:
Others---"How blest the Paradise to come!"
Ah, take the Cash in hand and waive the Rest;

Oh, the brave Music of a distant Drum!

So I returned to India ready to resume my previous life there and I quickly picked up where I had left off. It was amazing how rapidly I was back in the old routine. Joan Biddlesworth welcomed me back with enthusiasm and listened most attentively to a carefully edited account of my doings in England. I ignored the hints from her married sister that as I was spending time with Joan that I might like to put our relationship upon a more permanent footing. But it was all soon to be changed, for by 1853 it was clear that at some time we would be at war with Russia, and I was told to ready myself to go wherever I would be most useful.

I was not surprised therefore when the Russian War was well under way to be recruited to take my part in it. I was unprepared however for the way in which I was to be used. I was called in, I won't say by whom, and asked if I was prepared to accompany a certain Captain Nolan who had asked for someone to assist him. He had been told that he was to go to the Crimea but was first to collect more horses because the way that the whole campaign was being run so far meant that both men and horses were dying by the hundreds.

"Captain Nolan has made a request for someone to accompany him who is good with horses and good with languages too. We know that you have these qualities and have done sterling work with the Thuggee and Dacoitry Department", I was told.

"But the East India Company will not last forever. I expect you have realised that. This piece of work will give you the opportunity to expand your experience so as to take part in what ever takes its place."

I hesitated. My hesitation was not about the work but about Captain Nolan. As I have already told you we met in London. He was a snob of the very worst kind; and as he himself was looked down on himself by the regular officers in the British Army as an officer who served in India, you might have thought he would have been more sympathetic to those under him. Not a bit of it! I knew from that time that I had met him and from what others had told me that he would consider himself so superior to me that he would humiliate me on a regular basis.

I was right. That is exactly how things turned out. I was however, as you may have gathered by now, engaged in other less open duties than those that I regularly manifested. I knew that this appointment would give me opportunities to expand my knowledge and contacts, both of which would make me so much more useful, so I accepted what would not be a pleasant posting; it would instead be a hard slog. What I was effectively engaged in has been described as 'The Great Game' but I can tell you - it is no game. I bought a copy of Nolan's book: The Training of Cavalry Remount Horses: A New System, 1852, packed it along with my other kit and reported for duty.

It was a hard slog when we both arrived at Turkey. The exact place does not matter for we necessarily moved around in our quest for remounts. The hard work was all mine of course for Captain Nolan never let me forget his rank and told me quite early on that he had only taken on this task as a means to get into the war where he hoped to distinguish himself and show the British Army that Indian Officers were infinitely superior to their British counterparts. It says a great deal of course that it was an Indian Officer who was sent to collect remounts. I very much doubt whether any British Officer would have been given such a lowly task. One of the thoughts that kept me going at this time was what might happen to Captain Nolan when we did get to the Crimea. I suspected that some work with horses or provisions might be involved and I am human enough to have wanted to see him taken down a peg or two.

In the meantime Captain Nolan, who had spent a considerable sum in purchasing his captaincy, was not going to sully his hands with horse coping thank you very much; that was left to me. My first task was to find him an attendant. I found a rascally Moslem lad who not only waited upon Nolan but taught me some of the local dialects, and most useful of all, kept me informed as to Nolan's whereabouts and activities. He was also extremely useful for he seemed to have an inexhaustible collection of 'cousins' on whom he could call as we increased our stock of horseflesh. His other merit was in obtaining meals that were edible but still exotic. I pride myself on my robust digestion, but even I have to be careful.

What a shock awaited Captain Louis Edward Nolan when we arrived in the Crimea. Much as I expected he was assigned to duties related to the horses that we had brought, despite having been assigned as ADC to Brigadier-General Richard Airey, for Airey was Lord Raglan's quartermaster-general in the campaign. Being involved in the quartermastering side of things was certainly not to his taste so Nolan offered himself as an interpreter between the British and the French. I think that he also did this to get into Mrs Duberly's circle for she seemed to have a great deal of influence. She largely ignored him however. She had too many other fish to fry. I heard later about the book that she had written. In this missive she tried to assert that she was the only woman who had been there throughout the whole campaign! Naturally she discounted the wives of the troops, but even so she was wrong. Being ignored by a paymaster's wife didn't stop Nolan though for he soon got himself an invitation to Lord Cardigan's Yacht where he obtained an agreement that despite his work as ADC to Brigadier-General Richard Airey he could still be included in some real soldiering.

Well, we all know how that turned out, don't we. Now if you plead ignorance here of the famous charge I can only suggest you read Tennyson's poem. I must say that I was less shocked to hear of his death(Nolan's not Lord Tennyson's) than that of Calvert who was the head of the Secret Intelligence Department of the army. I had made it my business to meet him of course. Luckily they had Charles Cattley who had not long since been expelled out of the British Council at Kertch to take on some of Calvert's duties. I never met him because I was called back to India. I didn't meet William Howard Russell either, I'm glad to say. It's all very well writing scurrilous stuff for the common herd, but I think he went too far. I'm sure that he caused that riot in Trafalgar Square where near on two thousand people gathered to protest about the war and began to pelt buses with snowballs. It all got out of hand, and soon cabs and even people who were watching were the target of the rioters. Even the police were not immune to attack. I'm glad to say though that the police and soldiers put a stop to it all eventually. You have to nip these outbreaks in the bud.

Chapter 8

1855

An army marches on its stomach.

I heard in the mess one evening that they were all going down to the British Hotel later on. I had heard about this establishment that was apparently run by a black woman who had somehow managed to get herself out to the war in order to make money. Of course she could not have done it without the aid of a man. Women simply do not have that sort of ability. He was a Mr Day, a shadowy figure. I never met him. Well, we all repaired to this hostelry that I had previously heard was a sink of corruption, according to Miss Nightingale. We were welcomed by a large jolly West Indian woman who was indeed Mary Seacole, the black business woman of whom I had heard. I looked in vain for a Mr Seacole, suspecting that he did not exist but I did see a young black girl, Sally, who came to take our orders for what was surprisingly well cooked food.

In my usual way I struck up a conversation with one of the enlisted men there who was scarcely able to contain his praise for Mrs Seacole, or Mother Seacole as he styled her. She not only ran this place he told me, but also went out onto the battlefields to help with the wounded. I expressed some doubt about this story at which my soldier became rather angry, no doubt due to the fact he had been able to get some alcohol.

"You officers don't do nothing for us soldiers, leaving us to die, but she ain't like that and you can ask any of my mates and they will all tell you the same, she's a angel, a real angel."

This tribute was accompanied by an angry waving of arms and not a few crumbs of bread ejected from his mouth from a loaf that my soldier had been eating. The fracas attracted Mrs Seacole,s attention and she came over to see what all the commotion was about.

I stood up and introduced myself saying that I had heard great things about her and her activities.

"Well now, Mr Driscoll. I call you mister on account of the fact that I don't see no badges of rank on you despite that you got on some sort of uniform. You tell me that you have heard things about me. Not from that Miss Nightingale I 'spect unless it's somethng bad. I did want to work with her, but I'm afraid that particular lady don't want me."

She eased her not inconsiderable frame down onto a chair.
"As you can see, the rush is over so I can spare some time to have a little chat with you."

She gave mild look at the soldier who took the obvious hint and stumbled away. She saw my disapproving look at his gait and said:

"No, he is not drunk, but it is difficult to walk with only one foot you know."

I felt my face begin to go red. I felt hot. I took off my jacket mumbling something about it being warm inside. She smiled a sunny forgiving smile and said:

"Now I understand that there are a few questions that you would like me to answer."

"Oh Mrs Seacole. That sounds so very formal. But I am so very curious you know."

"Yes. I heard that you are known for it, asking questions that is. Well, fire away!"

" They call you Mother Seacole."

"They call me that because that's what I try to be for these poor boys. They miss their mothers you know. Even those young officers do. When I was in Jamaica I gained a reputation for being someone who cared for the troops. Yes, I know very well what peoples say: that I'm only here to make money. Of course Mr Day and me have to make money. How else we going to be here and to help? That Miss Nightingale didn't want me. None of those proud women in England in their respectable committees wanted me so me and Mr Day came by ourselves. And look, I provide food and drink and medicine. I go out and I provide succour to those poor boys who are dying."

"I hear that you give them brandy."

"Yes I do. And if you were at death's door lying out in the cold, what you rather I did: knock on that door so that you can pass on quickly, or give you something to ease your way?"

It was Mrs Seacole's turn to be heated. I waited until she regained her composure which she did almost immediately. I then heard most of her story of how she had managed to get to Balaclava which I can only describe as remarkable. She said that prior to coming to the Crimea her experiences had fitted her uniquely for the role that she now played. She added that sadly those fine ladies on their committees in London had not wished for her to come here. It was because of this that she took some pleasure in telling me about Dr James Barry. He was the Inspector-General Surgeon who had the strangest squeaky voice and the most peculiar mincing manner of walking. She got up to demonstrate his walk that provoked such a roar of appreciation from all the men that she sat down immediately.

Despite his voice and manner he was a real tartar and when he came to Miss Nightingale's hospital in Scutari he really laid into her about the conditions there. Miss Nightingale said afterwards that he was the most hardened creature that she had ever met in the whole time that she had been in the army. Her opinion of him was that he was a brute. I learned much later that he had no business being in the Crimea, but had used his leave to go to see for himself the truly dreadful conditions for he was, in his way, a reformer.

Mrs Seacole intrigued me, for despite having the assistance of a white man, Mr Day, I still could scarcely believe that a black woman, albeit one that was not that dark, could have accomplished all that she, and others, said that she had. Then it came to me. I cross-examined her about her parents and she willingly owned that her mother, a Jamaican woman had married a Scottish officer. So that was the explanation; it was clearly from her father that she had inherited the ability to be so very successful. You see how the white supremacy will always show itself.

With this in mind I now felt much easier as she described to me her manifest activities. She certainly knew how to cook which was hardly strange for that is undoubtedly a feminine activity. Left to my own devices I have to say that I was helpless in that area and would probably starve. Naturally in India I had a man as a cook, but he was fit only to prepare native dishes unless pressed to do otherwise with very variable results.

"Well," I finally told her for I knew that everyone likes to be flattered.

"The food that I have had today was excellent."

She smiled complacently at my compliment.

"If it pleased Msieur Soyer I'm sure that it should also please you for he has consistently praised my poor efforts."

I must own that I was taken aback for while simple cooking is women's work, preparing food as a chef, can only really be done by a man and I knew that Alexis Soyer was pre-eminent in that profession. How could Mrs Seacole know this famous chef? I must have shown my confusion as I asked:

"Not *the* Alexis Soyer ?"

For she laughed and said:

"Yes indeed *the* Alexis Soyer, the chef who went to Ireland during the potato famine and helped to feed the starving masses with a soup kitchen. He has been here helping to feed the troops. Have you seen the field kitchen that he invented? It's a real marvel, although I should not like to have to rely on it cooking so much as I do. Now you were extremely lucky to have been served chicken and pork today."

She closed her eyes and leaning back only as far she was able, because her amplitude forbade too much of that kind of activity, she said dreamily:

"I well remember in 1853 when I was in Escribanos, where I was with the gold prospectors, that the natives there wanted us to eat monkeys. I just could not do it. What civilised person could be doing with pulling out of a pot a piece of bone that resembled a brown baby's limb? I tried parrots, so tough, and even squirrel, but nothing but nothing is the equal of chicken that has been well roasted. I can tell you, you were very lucky today."

I could do nothing but agree with her. I had eaten marvellously. My buttons were strained as a consequence, and were I only to be by myself, by now I would have undone a few. What had finished me off was her rice pudding. I told her that in India the English demand of their cooks such delicacies as bread and butter pudding and rice pudding. But never ever had I such a delicious rice pudding as she had served up today. It was truly superb.

She beamed and said:

"Now that is something that you really do not need to say for I can tell you that when it is rice pudding day they come from miles around for some of it."

"Mrs Seacole", I said, "when this war is over I do hope that you will take the time to set down most of the things that you have told me today."

She laughed that merry laugh of hers and told me that she very much doubted that she would have the time, besides, she added, she had never been that good at putting down her thoughts. I told her that she could surely find someone who would write down what she told them. She made no answer to this remark, but looked thoughtful as she got up and walked away, and I could see that my suggestion might just have lodged in her mind. I know now that it did for she did indeed go on to write a book that was immensely successful.

Thanks to some very kind friends who sent me a copy I was able to read 'Wonderful Adventures of Mrs Seacole in many lands' when it was published in July 1857. It was delightful to see a picture of her on the front of the book where the artist had caught her to perfection.

I had to wait a little later to read Mrs Duberly's book, and was keen to do so for my interest had been kindled by the parody of it in Punch. My interest had also been aroused by a rumour about Mrs Duberly's activities in the Russian war; it was thought by some that these activities were so very odd for the wife of a paymaster that she must have been in fact a spy for Russia! All nonsense of course, but it did not stop a file being opened on her by the appropriate authorities. By the way, I threw away Nolan's book.

Chapter 9

1855-1858

In rolling down the roads of time
On steely way that hums and sings
Faster goes the train;
But faster still the change it brings

With the death of Nolan I was recalled to India where it was now deemed important to have me involved in the growing spread of the railways in India. I had met Thomas Brassey in the Crimea who had been instrumental in providing a successful railway up from Balaclava Harbour to the front. He was there with some others who had been involved in getting the railway built. It was no end of a fine example of what the British could do once you had set aside such matters as class distinction. Not that I ever suffered from that. Of course others who were better connected than I was made it to the top much quicker. But slowly and surely I was moving up.

The great thing about Thomas Brassey was that he did what he said he was going to do. He and the others offered to build that railway at cost and they did so bringing out an army of navvies and all the necessary supplies and equipment in order to finish it in under eight weeks! What about that then? Can you imagine the British army doing anything so rapidly? And, do remember this was in the depths of winter. I suppose that my reports that I sent back about this helped them decide that railways were just the thing that India needed. Of course we needed skilled men with some go in them who were unlike the easy going blacks if the railways were to be successful.

Luckily we had in India a group who seemed to have been born for such a task. These were the Anglo-Indians whose part European background made them ideal. Cut off from both Europeans and Indians they immediately found their place in the railways.

It wasn't easy to get Brassey because he was so infernally busy in every direction that you could imagine. He worked all over Europe with that wife of his doing the translation when it was needed. In the end he was inveigled into helping with the Delhi railway. That meant a hundred thousand tons of rolling stock and materials and equipment had to be brought over from England. That was Brassey's style; he gloried in completing what others baulked at. It wasn't completed until 1864 so I am getting a bit ahead of myself here.

I guessed on my return to India that when we had beaten Russia at the Crimea there could be a complete switch in direction in our efforts to keep Russia out of India. There, I've said it. I have up to now only hinted at my other real purpose in India. Now you know what occupied me apart from my overt activities. What? You guessed that already? What clever chaps you are to be sure! Almost as clever as Joan Biddlesworth who had managed to become employed secretly by the Department. How had this happened? It was on account of her sister's husband being bought out. So many below him had tired of waiting for promotion and had therefore clubbed together to get the wherewithal to purchase his release. He had gone back to England to live in Cirencester, and Joan, appalled at the idea of being buried in that backwater, had worked on Major Smith to stay in India by getting herself into his household.

On the face of it she was merely another female with no role other than that of a firenghi memsahib who scolded the bearers and dhobi wallahs, but I found out that she did have a role other than that of an indolent memsahib. This is the way I found out: I had gone as normal to the office; I had stepped outside my bungalow as usual dropping some small coins, a few pice only into the sadhu's empty begging bowl as was my wont. My servants always approved of my doing so, saying that any good action in this world brought a reward. They were sure that by this action I acquired merit. I doubted that maxim very much, just as I used to doubt the avowal that all our prayers are answered. I say that I used to doubt it until Joan pointed out to me that of course they were all answered, but not always with the answer that we desired. So up to now everything was as normal. Then it became unusual.

I had gone in to see Major Smith, who by the way used this name and rank to cover his real name, and found Joan Biddlesworth looking at some papers on his desk. The tats were down to keep the office cool so it was shady but I could still see her clearly with papers in her hands. Alarmed at this sight, I said sharply:

"What are you doing here?"

She looked at me steadily not at all abashed at being caught handling sensitive papers in what was manifestly an area that was totally a man's preserve.

"Just what I am supposed to be doing."

Her sheer effrontery amazed me. Did she consider that because we had a sort of friendship that she could take such liberties? I asked coldly:

79

"And that is?"

With a smile that at the very least could only be described as supercilious, and certainly one that bordered on impertinence, she replied:

"You had better ask Major Smith that."

Then she gathered up an armful of maps and papers and, before I could stop her, swept out.

"Oh! Manfred", said the Major when I went to him immediately to deal with this breach of security,

"You have no idea how useful Joan has been to us."

'Joan useful'? I thought.

"Ever since that bad outbreak of fever when we lost Frazier and nearly lost George Thomas, she has taken on and done the work of both those men and..."

Here his voice dropped as if we were in danger of being overheard so much that I had to strain to listen. Now I am not a vain man but I do pride myself on retaining all my faculties, but if people will persist in mumbling...Exasperated I moved closer to him as he all but whispered:

"She has revolutionised the work. I expect that you are aware that she has a brilliant analytical mind?"

"Aha! Well. Yes. Of course as I have known her so long I have always been struck by her wide range of interests you know."

"And mathematics is only one of them."

Stunned at this amazing statement I could only say:

"Quite."

"Mathematics?" I said to Joan once I had found her in the little room that had been assigned to her.

"In all the time that I have known you mathematics has never ever figured as a subject between us. You never ever mentioned figures."

"Why should I have? We had so many other topics in common. Why should I have mentioned figures when I could listen to you telling me at length about your exciting experiences in London and so on?"

Of course. That was it. My exploits in the past had so dazzled her that she had been shy of mentioning that she had been forced to explore some arcane subject to keep herself from being bored. But she had however somehow used her information to impress the Major and I dearly wished to hear more from her how she had done it. I could tell from her smile that she knew that I wanted to hear more and I knew that I would have to give in and ask her outright so I said:

"How did you get started?"

She accepted my capitulation magnanimously and replied:

"It began with my reading an article that had been translated from the Italian by lady Byron, Lord Byron's daughter. She added notes to make it more intelligible and somewhat to my surprise I not only found that I understood it but I also enjoyed it. After that I badgered people to get me similar articles and books. Does the name Babbage and his difference machine mean anything to you?

I shook my head in negation. I knew about Lord Byron of course who had written all those poems that no one reads any more. I didn't know about his daughter though nor this Babbage fellow. Joan shook her head in exasperation, then began to enlighten me. After an hour we adjourned to the veranda of major Smith's household. There she continued to baffle me, both at the complexity of what she was telling me and how it might assist us.

Our people spent a great deal of their time going into those largely unmapped areas where instead of charts with vague mountains and valleys being shown they came back with more precise maps which owed as much to their skills as to their sheer physical slog. They had not only to plot accurately what they found but also to depict it in a flat media. Too much detail was as bad as too little; selection to reduce complexity was the key. So their skills had to be of the highest, and this included working out figures that in England would be done by people called computers.

Now this was where Joan really moved from reality into fantasy. She tried to tell me that lady Byron had worked on this fellow Babbage's adding machine and had improved it so much that it could do more complicated work. She had to admit that such a machine was theoretical. She then told me that it was Indian theory that had been brought to England in 1825 that had influenced Babbage. That did not amaze me for I had seen the Jantar Mantar at Jaipur. I have to admit however that I found it hard to accept her prediction that in time more sophisticated machines would be developed. I had seen natives using an abacus at such speed that no machine would ever challenge! I judged it prudent to keep my doubts to myself however; Joan seemed to have found a niche in the Department so did it matter if she had a few strange ideas? It kept her happy.

Now I am sure that you will have heard about the native uprising in India in 1857 and may have asked yourself why were we not forewarned? I have to say that we were. Some of us knew from signs that were unmistakable to us that trouble was being prepared. We held back, reluctant to act until we were sure of who was really behind these preparations. Then, when we had some hard evidence we were not believed. Those officers who commanded Indian regiments simply refused to accept that their sepoys and their subildars would rise against us. It was useless to argue with such stubborn refusal to accept the facts as we were able to present them.

Why did it happen? Well so much comes down to religion. And you cannot simply ignore what it was that the Indian troops were being told by people who were part of their long history. It also did not help that in some cases some of the sepoys had been treated so badly by the British lower ranks. And, I must be honest those soldiers were sometimes the sweepings of those cities in England whose honest burghers were grateful that they had gone into the army. I am quite certain that when the uprising came lots of outstanding scores were settled bloodily.

Of course, once the uprising was put down those who were strongest in their denial that their troops could be disloyal often became the ones that exerted the most appalling acts of punishment. And for a time I myself was in danger of such punishment.

I had attempted to do what I could to prevent mutiny as it broke out and as a result I found myself at Lucknow on the 26th of September.   I was fighting alongside a pitifully small band of men, one of whom was James Hollowell. There were just nine of us defending a burning house that we were inside. Later on I was able to attest to his courage, not that I needed to for others had this matter in hand and he was eventually awarded the Victoria Cross for his heroism. I was one of the 'dispirited men' that is mentioned in the citation. My prior attempts to prevent mutiny however were seen by some as being part of the mutiny. My close connection with certain Indians was taken as proof that I too had been disloyal. It still is not possible at this time to explain just how and why I was involved. Nor can I say why at this point my superiors chose to stay aloof from my predicament.

Luckily James Hollowell stood up for me, and hero that he was, they listened to him. I was able to return to my former duties with a promise from him that were he ever to get to the point that he could retire to England he would welcome me right royally should I ever be there on leave. Many such fine promises are made of course, but this one was to be kept with surprising consequences.

It was at this time that I also ran across Mrs. Duberly again for she had accompanied her husband when the 8th Hussars were sent to India in 1856 and she stayed with him throughout the whole of the time that he was involved with the

Indian mutiny. I have to admit that she was game one. I was with her afterwards on a hot and steamy afternoon when she said that she was going to write to her sister to tell her that she stained her face and hands and put on native clothes in order to prevent being left behind when the regiment went into action. She was so determined to be there with the troops that she got her bearer to supply her with a turban and caftan. The turban hid her hair and the caftan, being loose, hid her figure. I was not surprised to hear this for she had already delighted in recounting to me how in the Russian war she had fooled Lord Raglan who had forbidden her to embark with the troops. She had disguised herself then as a native woman on an ox cart, had it driven to the Himalaya and got herself smuggled on board. When I asked why she had taken such steps, she replied:

"I am married to a man who, if I am not constantly at his side, is taken advantage of to such an extent that he would quickly be ruined. It was my idea you know that he should study to be a paybob."

Being a paymaster kept him comparatively out of harm's way. It also increased his pay and gave him a simpler way of achieving promotion. Actually I already knew the story of her in the Himalaya for it was there in her file that come to India; it was sent out as there was still some doubt about her being a spy for the Russians. I must say that the more I read about her dressing up to fool the authorities the more credence was leant to this theory. She was no Fanny Parkes though. She might on occasions dress up but she really had no real understanding of India and its many denizens.

By 1858 the East Indian Company was no more. Disraeli, Queen Victoria's favourite Prime Minister, put it down like an old dog that has had its time and created an empire instead with the Queen as Empress of India. No wonder he was her favourite Prime Minister! Apparently she was delighted to be an Empress as she had relatives who were Emperors so she now was as good as them. I found little changed, apart from names and posts. The Thuggee and Dacoitry Department still existed. I had returned to it and found Forbes-Bosely was also there. I now thought now that I was safe from him as my involvement in my sub-rosa activities meant that I was protected. He was fatter, bloated rather, but still quite handsome in a dark fleshy way and still of the opinion that he was important and I was not. I never challenged his opinion, not of himself nor of me. Just now and then I caught him looking at me in a puzzled way. I was still wary of him despite my protection. You will see that I was right to be.

Meanwhile Joan Biddlesworth was now embedded in the Department to such an extent that were I to be a jealous man I might have been envious of the ease of access she had to those who directed our operations. But, bearing in mind that she was only a woman, albeit one whose mind nearly approached that of a man, I would have laughed at anyone who might have presumed that I held her in envy. Nonetheless, it was a certain twinge of some sort of emotion that I felt as I passed her working on heaven knows what to go in to see Major Smith. He had asked me to come in early as he had something to impart.

"What do you know about Australia?"

"Not a lot sir. I know we used to send our criminals there, from England that is."

"Well, you won't need to know much more than that. But this assignment that I'm giving you is about that antipodean country."

I tried to look intelligent and interested, but to tell you the truth I was more interested in what Joan was dealing with in the outer office.

Chapter 10

1858 –1860

God made the horse, but the camel was designed by a committee

Ignoring me, the Major looked distastefully at the papers that were before him.

"I think it's all going to be a waste of time, but who am I to query my masters?"

I waited. The Major often rambled on like this. It was his method of getting his thoughts in order.

"It's this chap Landells. Funny fellow. Came to India in '42 then fetched up in Australia. He has now come back with a commission to buy camels if you please. They are to be shipped to Melbourne for some dam' fool expedition."

He rustled through his papers.

"Apparently, apparently, they want to go from Melbourne straight up to the top of Australia, and as they know there's desert in the hinterland they think it will be best to use camels. It seems that the Government is supporting this scheme."

It was time to ask an intelligent question.

"So why is the The Thuggee and Dacoitry Department involved?"

"You might well ask. Good question actually. It seems that the India Office is worried about this chap Landells. They are all twitchy still because of the uprising. He was in India before it, and we don't know much about him or what he was doing here. Anyway he's here again, came on the Gertrude. Now, what I want you to do is go to Kolkata and get to know him. You can tell him that the army has given you leave and you are spending it in India as you ain't got anyone to spend it with in England."

He looked at me sharply.

"That bit's true ain't it?"

I nodded.

"Offer to help him. We are making it difficult behind the scenes, so you can say that you might be able to assist him. Once you've gained his trust we will ease up. Go with him then to buy his camels and do the usual reports."

It was not at all difficult to get to know George Landells. I just made sure that we ran into each other in Kolkata. Almost before he knew anything about me he was telling me about his problems.   I heard at length about his commission to buy camels and I simulated such interest in why he was purchasing them that he insisted on buying me a drink and telling me the whole tale. I made sure that we met again and when I did so he said:

"I say, you must have brought me luck. They say that I can go ahead and travel up to Lahore. I'm told that you get the best beasts in the North."

He really was naïve for when I said that I had always wanted to see something of North India and offered to join him his face glowed, what one could see of it that is, for he had a moustache and beard to rival any Sikh. I asked him once jokingly whether he was not secretly an Indian. He took my query seriously.

"Oh no, I could never be. I'm much too fair."

So we travelled together to buy his camels. As we went up country he told me about the camels that he wanted to buy. I tried to draw him out on his past life but he was curiously reticent and whenever we got on to that subject he shied off it like a horse that sees a snake.

In Lahore he had to modify his ideas about which breeds he wanted to buy. I watched him as he set about bargaining. He was pathetic. In the end I stepped in and said to the filthy rascal who was trying to sell him some broken down old camels that really should have been shot:

"You dirty misbegotten son of a whore. Take those filthy things that you pretend are camels and bring us some real ones. Go!"

George Landells looked stricken. I have never before seen a grown man actually wring his hands together, but now I actually saw that happen.

"Oh please come back", he pleaded to the back of the offended salesman. Raj Dal beside me actually chuckled until I gave him a stern look.

"What am I going to do now? He said that he was the only dealer here who was supposed to deal with Europeans."

"George. Do you always believe everything that anyone tells you? That man has bought off the other dealers so that he can sell you those half dead specimens. He will then share what he makes with them."

I had a sudden suspicion.

"George, you didn't tell him how much you had to spend did you?"

He blushed. I groaned. Raj Dal now openly laughed. I glared at him. He stopped laughing and looked solemn.

"Right. Pack up now. We are going to Peshawar. And when we get there leave the dealing to Raj here.

In Peshawar Raj bought twenty-six camels, for half the sum that George was prepared to pay: eight large riding camels and eighteen pack animals. I told Landells that my leave was up so that I had to return to rejoin my regiment, but that I would leave Raj Dal with him. I said that Raj would help him with the sepoy camel handlers, and that he could trust him. Before I left I spoke to Raj Dal who was not at all worried at the prospect of walking nearly a thousand miles to Karachi. Before I could say a word he said that he knew exactly what I required, and we agreed a system where, if it was necessary, he would send word to me.

"Sahib Landells is a child in a man's body", was his parting words to me.

I hoped that he was right and that George Landells was not playing some sophisticated game with us. When they reached Karachi I went to see them. I had been told to delay them long enough to enable the Department to do some final enquiries. Raj Dal saluted me.

"Jai Ram Huzzoor. You see we are safely here, but two of the camels died."

Seeing my look he went on hastily that he had sold the dead camels for meat and that the money that he had got for it was more than the price that had been paid originally for the live camels. I waited. There was a pause. He said:

"As your honour knows, there is always a little extra."

I smiled.

"Then because we understand each other the little extra is yours", I said and turned to meet the remainder of George Landell's party which now was swollen to nine sepoys, John King, John Drakeford and George Landell's wife.

I was introduced to them all and invited to eat that evening with them.

"To tell you the truth Manfred I'm very pleased to see you because we seem to be stuck here. Every time I think we have managed to get away something else is mentioned. I tell you the number of bits of paper and chits of all sorts..."

I nodded sympathetically. I planned to see his wife on the quiet to see whether she could cast more light on him, so I said:

Well, I will see what I can do."

In the end I did not have to seek out Mrs Landells for she came to my room to see me. She came all swathed with a veil around her head. She unwrapped herself as if unwrapping a parcel and said:

"Please forgive me, but I am so terribly anxious about George. He's so trusting that I am sure that they will take advantage of him. He's desperately keen to join this expedition that he thinks that when he delivers the camels they will automatically give him a place. Actually, I am fairly sure that they will take him on, but it's the terms of his contract that worries me. You see, I know that where the are going is likely to be dangerous and I have to face the fact that he might not come back."

She pulled out a minute handkerchief releasing a scent that I suppose she would have described as a perfume, but I was merely a soldier and know little of such things so I breathed it in and kept quiet. She dabbed her eyes. She spoke in a low subdued voice.

"Please, do advise me. I can see that you have been such a help to George, and I do not suppose that had you not helped him that he would not have been so successful..."

Her voice trailed away as she once again placed that small fragment of cambric and lace to her eyes that sparkled with tears? How do I know that it was made of such substances you ask, seeing that I was merely a soldier? The truth is that before she left she dropped it and I picked it up, secreting it in an inner pocket.

"Why don't you suggest to him that he writes a letter saying how much he expects to be paid. He could also put in it a suggestion that if, God forbid! he does perish in this hazardous enterprise, they should pay you a sum of say, twice the yearly salary he is to get. In that way you get to strike the first blow as it were."

"Yes, thank you, that seems to be an eminently sensible idea. I cannot tell you how you have relieved my mind."

She laid a hand momentarily upon mine in thanks. I was touched at her regard for her husband. She then lingered long enough for me to gather some salient facts about her him, all of which seemed to support my view that he was exactly as he presented himself: a rather simple dealer in horses and camels. Indeed he had apparently supplied us with considerable numbers of Walers in the past. Those horses always seemed to do well in India. Mrs Landells said in effect that when it came to horses and camels her husband's knowledge and understanding were outstanding.

"I only wish he had as much nous about people", she sighed as she wrapped her veil about her and left me. I resumed my cigar. It was then that I saw that she had dropped her handkerchief.

I now have to admit that had not meant to tell Joan about this encounter but she literally sniffed it out. We were wrapping up some loose ends about this episode when she suddenly said:

"What's that smell?"

I tried to feign innocence, but she seized my coat, delved into my inner pocket and drew out Mrs Landells' handkerchief.

"Aha! This is not the usual rag that you keep about your person to attend to your nose. And it is sweetened with something better than attar of roses, unless I am considerably mistaken."

I tried to snatch it back. She backed away, waved it at me provocatively and demanded the full story. Actually she knew most of it already for she told me later on that Mrs Landells and I had been seen that evening and were already the subject of a supplementary report which she had read and filed!

When I had finished my version of what had taken place between Mrs Landell and myself, Joan laughed. To be candid this was not the reaction that I had expected so I naturally demanded an explanation.

"Oh you silly, silly man. Do you really not know why Mrs Landells dropped her handkerchief?"

And that was all she would say.

It was in 1863 when I heard about the way the Burke and Wills expedition had finally turned out to be a disaster. Luckily George Landells had withdrawn from it over some argument to do with the camels, so he did not die as all the others did, so Mrs Landells didn't lose him. Actually, now I remember, there was a survivor. It was John King. I had met him just before George Landell set off in the Chinsurah with those camels. George had collected him and John Drakeford along with the sepoy camel drivers. I wonder what became of them? He, John King that is, was saved by some native aboriginal girl who took him into her tribe. He lived with her and then abandoned her and the daughter that he had fathered. It was a similar tale that I often heard when English soldiers went back to England leaving behind them native Indians and half-caste children.

I tried at least once more to find out from Joan just what she had meant about Mrs Landells, but she always refused to say another word upon that matter. When I pressed her she would change the subject of our conversation, sometimes drawing my attention to something that had interested her to divert my attention. In was in this fashion that she showed me an American paper where there was a report about a phenomenon that had intrigued her. I was by now accustomed to her wide-ranging interests; nothing seemed too outlandish for her not to seize upon it. I had also learned that she usually had some ulterior motive for taking an interest in something.

On this occasion what she showed me was about the telegraph machine, that apparatus that made it possible in the Russian war to send home reports by that dreadful journalist who inflamed the public so.

TELEGRAPH GOES WILD

Across the United States of America reports have been flooding in of strange events where electricity from an unknown source seems to have affected the telegraph machinery so much that it had to be shut down for safety's sake. In one case that was reported the machinery carried on although it had been switched off. Apparently it was being powered by electricity in the air. In another case the electricity was so

97

powerful that it burned out the wires. No one has been able to say yet where this force of electricity came from...

"This is not all. I have since found that there is an astronomer, a Richard Carrington, who says that these events are all caused by flares that have come out from the sun that have upset all the electrical appliances. He discovered what he has called solar flares. You do see how important this is don't you?"

"Not really."

She made an impatient gesture.

"It means that were this to happen we could be at risk of being attacked when we were struggling with dealing with our lack of means of communication."

"Now Joan are you not in danger of letting your imagination run away with your wits?"

This time her impatient gesture was followed by a refusal to speak to me for weeks; a situation that put paid completely to my asking her again about Mrs Landells. It was her loss though for I had meant to tell her about the Burke and Wills expedition in some detail as I had taken the trouble to read about it, and therefore could have given her hours of pleasure.

Chapter 11

1862

As it was Eve who caused young Adam's fall
And Pandora who let slip troubles all
So men, prepare to run some miles
When women start to use their wiles

The spring of 1862 brought an invitation from James Hollowell to attend his wedding. I imagine that he thought that I would not be able to get to England for it, but I pulled a string or two and intimated that a spell in England might allow me to cobble together a coterie of individuals that could be useful in our work so I was granted some leave.

I stayed with Jack Whicher in Holywell Street as it was Whicher's niece, Sarah who was to be married from there. She was marrying James Hollowell who was Charlotte Piper's nephew; Charlotte Piper being Jack Whicher's landlady. I took the liberty of introducing the subject of the Road Hill House Murder for I had read Stapleton's book on the subject and I was curious to know from Jack Whicher's own lips what he thought about the whole business. I might as well of asked the wall for all the answers that I got. Whicher was apparently as adept in keeping mum as he was in solving crimes. He did surprise me though. Somehow he knew something of my activities. He did not quiz me about them, but merely let me understand that he knew someone who had spoken to someone and so on. The upshot of this was an invitation to Scotland Yard after the wedding to see someone whom I might care to meet.

All this was in the context of the worries that the Police in London had had following the death of Prince Albert. The funeral had presented a unique opportunity to foreigners to make trouble and gain notoriety. In particular there were concerns about Moslems. It seemed that there were several in England in an organisation that the police kept an eye on as they thought they might attempt an assassination. I was not actually told so, but it was intimated to me that several secret arrests had had to have been made just prior to the funeral.

Whicher told me that there were worries too about possible attempts upon the life of the queen. There had already been a few. In 1850 the Queen was actually injured by an ex-army officer, Robert Pate. Whicher told me that he had attacked her with a cane. Luckily he inflicted no more damage than smashing in her bonnet giving her a bruised head. It was probably because she was only bruised that he was only sentenced to seven years' transportation. It could also be because he was ex-army. There was some talk at the time that his mind was disturbed. Whicher said that in his career he had come across quite a few such poor souls. I too had met some whose minds following military action had become unhinged. Some merely went to pieces, as it were, becoming mere shells of their former selves. Others developed a fixed idea about some wrong and proceeded to try to right it with some inappropriate activity, like Robert Pate.

The wedding was not a grand affair. The couple were married quickly in a church whose name escapes me. Perhaps as I continue to tell my story it will come back. Afterwards we went to a public house where on the upper floor we had the wedding breakfast with a bride cake that I thought a trifle too grand for the small number of guests. Most were relatives of the bride. James Hollowell's guests were mainly old comrades and as he had lost so many in past skirmishes and battles they were necessarily few in number. What they lacked in numbers they made up in boisterousness though, and twice we had mine host coming upstairs as he thought we had fallen to fighting, for the noise we made was so great it resembled a miniature battle. I enjoyed it. It was good to be amongst fine honest men whose principles were similar to mine, if you ignored their propensity to looting; but how else is a serving soldier to keep fed and try to provide for his old age, supposing that it that he ever gets there?

The following day Whicher gave me an address in Pimlico where he said I might find someone who would like to meet me. He brushed aside what he had said previously about a meeting in Scotland Yard and winked as he repeated that this mysterious personage would much better serve my ends. Before I went he said that I should go to see Elizabeth Butler's famous picture. 'Remnants of an Army' that showed William Brydon as the sole survivor of the terrible massacre of Elphinstone's Army, the East India Company of 4,500 troops. Of course it wasn't only the army that was annihilated, 12,000 civilian workers, family members and other camp-followers also perished.

Following his advice I did so and was reminded as I looked at William Brydon on his horse how everyone had thought at the time that he had been the only survivor. This was because only he had ridden in to the British garrison at Jalalabad. It became a legend that only he had survived out of thousands. I knew that this was not so. Several others had also escaped and straggled in later. Some legends refuse to die however, and just as at the beginning of the Russian War in the Crimea everyone thought that only Florence Nightingale was there caring for the soldiers and only later did it emerge that Mary Seacole had also been a Crimean war heroine, so did this idea of a single survivor persist. Looking at the picture, I could see why.

Looking at the scrap of paper that Whicher had given me I took a cab from outside the gallery, gave the address to the cabbie and was taken to a most unsavoury district not far from the Millbank Penitentiary. I went inside what seemed to be house, only to find that it was in fact an office where I encountered a man who was badly scarred by frostbite and answered to the name that Whicher had given me. He listened politely as I told him that James Whicher had suggested that we meet, then proceeded to explain to me that he had been one of those who had escaped from the Kabul massacre in 1842. He was one of the officers that had been captured by Akbar Khan and so escaped death. When we revenged this terrible event and Sale rescued his wife Lady Sale, who had been a hostage, he and some other hostages were rescued.

"As you know by now, Brydon, when he answered the question 'Where is the army?' by saying "I am the army', he started a legend. In fact several more of us survived. I am Captain George Leach by the way I am most pleased to meet you. I must tell you that you will not find my name listed among the rescued officers. For reasons that will become apparent later I now have this new name."

It appeared that following Leach's return to England work had been found for him in this office; it was clerical work of the most boring and stultifying kind, dealing with dockets and missing lists of supplies and other soul destroying tasks. I could not but help saying that he must find it so very boring for he was manifestly an educated and intelligent man. He smiled at that and asked me to walk through into an inside office where having given me a glass of really excellent Maderia wine he said:

"I'm not surprised that you find what I seem to be engaged in each day to be so boring. Perhaps you will find this more interesting."

He rummaged around and produced a paper that he passed to me. It looked familiar. I unfolded it and was astounded to find that it seemed to be a copy of one of my own reports that was supposed to be highly confidential.

"How the devil did you come by this?" I asked.

"Oh we have our ways you know."

His calm reply was followed by a shout of laughter from him.

"Oh Manfred, Manfred, you should see your face."

He then explained that it had been decided that after the Kabul fiasco he should be used in military intelligence. The work on manifests etc was his cover. This was the reason that his name was changed. He went on to explain that up to now, although I too was to be included in such work it had seemed sensible to leave me unaware of the full extent of what went on. Now however he explained I was to be made privy to much more than I had been up to this time. In the next hour I was given a full explanation of how this section operated and was told that Sir Edward Bradford, to give him the short name that was used in this section, knew that I was coming to England and had arranged for this meeting.

"After 1842 it was decided that whatever happened we must do everything possible to frustrate the Russians. They will attempt to get into Afghanistan you know. They will not give up easily and from there they will try to take India from us. I am a small part in this huge engine that works day and night to stop them. In due course you will meet others that are either already in this work like you, or have been recruited."

He intimated that the work had spread beyond this worthy aim and now included dealing with attacks upon royalty. In essence he told me the gathering of intelligence was now so widespread it could and should be used more widely; there really was no limit to what we considered should come into our net, wherever it is, and whatever it is, we collect it.

I mulled over this statement that evening as I took a glass from a bottle of a damned fine port wine that had been given me as I left the London section. I was in the hotel that I had chosen to spend my last few days in England before returning to India, and I was of the opinion that as the Department was putting up the brass for my trip I saw no reason to skimp, so I had taken what they called a suite, a foreign word for some rooms rather than one. A maid tapped on the door and roused me from what was beginning to be my usual descent into a sleepy state that preceded a final tumble into bed.

"And it please you sir there is a lady below who desires to speak with you on a matter that she says is of the utmost importance."

I immediately assumed that somehow I was being contacted about a departmental matter. How stupid of me to make such an assumption; I can only now plead that having dined well and taken wine with my dinner of roast capon, then port wine, my defences were down.

"Please show her up."

The maid bobbed obediently and left and I attempted to gather my wits about me thinking that I would need to be ready for any new intelligence that might be imparted to me. The maid opened the door and the lady, veiled and mysterious, entered. She threw back her veil to reveal one of the handsomest faces that I have ever had the good luck to set eyes upon with dark eyes set in a pale face and surrounded by coal black hair that crept out from her bonnet.

"You know me not", she began as I took her outstretched gloved hand. The gloves were of the finest soft leather. They were all of a piece with her gown and her bonnet, and even I, a mere rough soldier, could see that her clothes spoke of her being a lady of the highest quality.

"But I know you, or rather I know of you for I have never yet had the pleasure of you having been introduced to me."

"Madam..." I replied.

"...it must be for me a matter of the utmost regret that we have never before chanced across one another as we are so happily met today."

"A pretty speech sir, but you speak without knowing what it is that I will be asking of you."

"Ask away", I replied recklessly. I assure you that it was the wine talking; had I not been punishing the port wine I might have been more circumspect. To my amazement she began to remove her outer and upper garments. Soon she stood before me clad only in her stays that revealed her pure white shoulders and the upper parts of her anatomy that I could name were I not a gentleman. She turned her back to me and said:

"There. You see how mercilessly I have been treated."

Indeed, across her back there were red weals that seemed to owe their origin to someone having punished her with a cane or some other instrument. I felt my face flame to a colour to match those stripes.

"They served me thus as I would not forswear my beliefs. I have other marks upon my body that I must give up my dignity as a lady in order to show you so as to impress you with the gravity of the absolute and utmost distress to which I have been driven. I came to you as someone who owns a conscience and will assist me in my hour of need. With that she removed her skirt and petticoat and would have also divested herself of her drawers had I not cried out:

"No! no! no more dear lady."

Now even I, credulous and good hearted, became suspicious for she at this very moment produced a whip from her reticule, saying:

"And this is the instrument that was used upon me. Take it, I implore you to feel how much I suffered from its laying on to my skin."

With that, she turned her back to me, bent over and despite my entreaties for her to cease, her drawers began to slide down for she had surreptitiously loosened the scarlet ribbon that held them in place. My face, already hot now burned hotter as I viewed the sight that was offered me.

Now I knew that were I foolish enough to grasp the whip I would be caught red-handed, for my handsome lady was...a trap! She was the bait. I was supposed to take the instrument of torture and when I did so she would cry out. When she had done so, in would rush her rescuers. I would be accused of ill-using a woman for my personal pleasure and she would sob piteously saying that I had persuaded her against her better judgement to accompany me in my suite to drink a glass of wine...and this was the result. It was a variation of the badger game, where a lady of easy virtue is caught in flagrante delicto with a gentleman by a man who pretends to be an outraged husband. In this case however, I was sure that it was not money that I would be asked for in compensation. No, I sensed that there was more behind this than cash. And sure enough, when I declined to touch the whip she screamed. And sure enough someone did barge in. And what a surprise when it turned out to be Forbes-Bosely. Of course I am being ironic. It was no surprise at all.

"Well, well, what have we here? he sneered."

The 'lady', her work done, gathered up her clothing and went into my inner room.

"This is not going to look well in my report" he went on.

"I shall deny it; those who know me will know that it is a base fabrication. It will be my word against yours."

"Ah! But I shall have not only my word but also that of the lady whom you have so cruelly treated to satisfy your disgusting desires."

This was a facer. I knew that this could mean the end of my career. Then to my amazement, Whicher and George Leach came out of the inner room along with my 'lady'. Somehow they had got wind of this plot and had entered my suite from the other side. Forbes-Bosely smiled.

"So you do have friends, Driscoll. Their evidence will not save you however when this young woman says her piece to the authorities."

"And what would that be?" she asked as she went past him and left the room, saying as she did so:

"I have never met this gentleman and know nothing of him"

I noticed, now that I was no longer distracted by her bare flesh, that her accent was decidedly that of one of the lower classes. Forbes-Bosely's face showed that he knew that he had been defeated.

"Why?" he shouted after her. "Why?"

"You did not pay her enough" laughed Leach. Jack Whicher smiled in agreement.

Chapter 12

1862

Tho' it was Eve who caused young Adam's fall
And Pandora who let slip those troubles all
To be wed is an honorable state
So close your eyes sir and embrace your fate

On my return to India I felt that I was now sufficiently advanced in my career and safe insofar that I had avoided most illnesses that men like me succumbed to, and was probably now immune to, so that I could contemplate marriage. It would also assist me to counter any further attacks on my good name were I to be wed.

I had seen so many marriages that were arranged only on the basis of what could be gained from such an alliance that I determined that I would choose my future wife regardless of her circumstances. It would not matter to me how rich or poor she was, nor was I going to be swayed by her station in life. Of course, it goes without saying that she would have to be a real lady. But I would not look for more than that.

Joan Biddlesworth completely agreed with my assessment. She was now a most valued colleague. She was quicker than any man that I have ever met at summing up a situation and presenting all the salient points. Kept in the background for forms sake she nevertheless dominated the thinking in the Department. She should have been a man; I told her this once and my comment was so patently true that she was moved to tears by it!

In time I found Caroline Hoostracht, a lady who met all my conditions. She immediately accepted my proposal of marriage as I had expected she would, for I was now well-established and of good reputation. Several of my colleagues congratulated me saying how lucky my new bride was to be married to me. It is truly gratifying to receive such compliments. Only a few expressed amazement that I had chosen such a young woman with little or no prospects. Actually I was able to disabuse them of this notion for Caroline's widowed mother had made a reasonable settlement upon her daughter which now came to me of course. I'm sure that I do not need to tell you that my wife was extremely grateful that I took over this sum and invested it wisely for she admitted to me candidly that, just like most women she really had no notion of numbers and financial matters. They really are so delightfully vague at times, but we have to forgive them do we not?

This last opinion was shared by her two brothers who were successful traders in India, exporting to Holland all sorts of spices and other goods that they were able to purchase cheaply through their contacts. It pleased them no end that their sister had had the good luck to be noticed by me. Of course they were equally pleased that she had married someone who had been employed by the old East Indian Company. That Company might have gone out of business now that Queen Victoria was Empress of India, but lots of sections remained which were concerned with trade; and trade was the life blood of the Empire. What did old Whatshisname say:

'The sinews of war are money,' or something similar.

Now come along. You really can't expect me to remember everything.

I do remember being asked though when I had returned to India before I got married whether I had enjoyed my leave in England. Apparently I amazed my questioner by saying that I had been disgusted at the poverty, the filth and squalor in London, and that the way the rich lived by lording it over the common man was enough to make any decent man upset. It was pointed out to me that I had just in fact described India. My reply to that was that Great Britain now had an Empire and should be setting an example.

I had seen in England, and I don't doubt for an instant that it was the same in the rest of the countries that made up Great Britain: rickets, poor housing, destitution, and starvation for the majority of the population. And all this in a civilised society alongside such outpourings of wealth as evidenced by the season when as much as would keep ten families fed and decently sheltered was spent in a single night on a party. I was reminded by Joan when I said the above that such parties meant that the poor were employed, to which I replied that indeed they were, only to be cast off when the season ended and the big houses were shut up. By the way I took good care not to invite Joan Biddlesworth to the wedding for she and Caroline were chalk and cheese and I knew that they would never get on together.

Now I come to a particularly painful part of my story for I'm afraid that I trusted my wife too much and she betrayed me, so I took what I considered to be a sensible way out of what would have been a disaster for both of us. Luckily I knew a hospital assistant who was stationed with the Central India Horse, which was a British cavalry regiment that I had connections with, and he took the boy and promised to bring him up as his own. Of course I did not tell my wife where the boy had been placed. I deemed that it was better that she knew nothing so that she could forget the whole disturbing incident. She went to Simla for a while and when she came back it was with the sad news that we told everybody that she had lost her new child to an outbreak of cholera.

I also considered that I should keep this whole matter as secret as possible. I did not even tell Joan Biddlecombe. There were occasions when I very nearly did so, but I closed my mind to the comfort of shared confessions. By now Joan had more or less given up wearing European clothing, preferring the comfort of native dress. One strange feature of this was the clothes that she wore; they were those worn by men! Indeed from the back she could easily have been taken for a babu.

Unknown to my wife I kept in touch with the hospital aide and by so doing I was able to keep track of his progress. Apparently he was a clever boy, learned fast and mastered languages easily, so that when I was again on leave in England he was already conversing in three languages. I went to England without my wife as I had a delicate task to undertake and I thought it prudent to tackle it by myself. I must add here that Caroline had not been as strong as I in putting to one side the unfortunate situation that her behaviour had occasioned, and she often fell into bouts of melancholy. These were then followed by equally disturbing weeks when her behaviour became hectic and alarming. The doctor that I consulted on her behalf about this thought it better that she should stay in India where she could be cared for by my household. He gave it as his opinion that a sea voyage and new surroundings might upset her. She needed to be kept calm and in a situation that was familiar to her. Speaking of doctors reminds me that one of the advantages of being employed as I was in the business of collecting information was that pieces of news that were supposed to be kept out of view were available to me. Thus I was fascinated to read of the death of Dr James Barry, the Inspector General of Military Hospitals.

I never met Dr Barry, but you might recall that Mrs Seacole, or Mother Seacole to so many, had told me about him and how Miss Florence Nightingale had found him to be 'a brute', so I was particularly intrigued by what I was now to read. Dr James Barry had been ill for some time and all those in attendance on him in his Cavendish Square home in London had found him to be as irascible as ever. When he died he was found the next morning in his bed by his cleaner, Sophia Bishop. He had given strict instructions that on no account were his clothes to be removed, and that he was to be buried in the clothes that were on him when he died. His cleaner disobeyed him and in so doing created a possible scandal. As she stripped him she found that not only was Dr James Barry a woman but, from marks that she observed upon her belly, she had given birth at some time!

This startling information was hidden away from the general public but the person who had ferreted it out found out a great deal more and it was all in the report that I now read.

Dr James Barry was born Margaret Buckley. A bright young woman, she took on the identity of her uncle who had died, and assisted by her mother, went to Edinburgh where she trained as a doctor disguised as a man. Lying about her age to excuse her lack of facial hair and always wearing bulky clothes she graduated three years later, moved back to London for a six-month stint as an apprentice surgeon at St Thomas's Hospital then in 1813, joined the Army. How amazing that surrounded by men in a men's world she still managed to keep her secret.

When in 1816 she was posted to South Africa she found a black manservant there who would stay with her for the next fifty years. She revealed her secret to him and he assisted her daily in her deception. Lord Charles Somerset, the governor of the colony became her close friend. He knew her secret and was a powerful ally whose protection must have helped to dispel any rumours about her. There was talk that Lord Charles was her lover. The fact that she was actually a brilliantly successful doctor helped no end for to ignore all the gossip and backbiting. Then around 1819 she disappeared for about a year. She claimed to have been sent to Mauritius, but what really happened was that she became pregnant and went away to give birth.

There was a great deal more, but I put it aside to read later. As I did so I thought to myself that even I, who was so used to deceptions of all kinds, was smitten with amazement at this story. How wonderful I thought that this pillar of the establishment, whose achievements included being the first doctor in England to perform a successful Caesarean delivery, was able to fool everyone for so long. I was able to show all the details about Dr James Barry, or rather Margaret Buckley, to Joan Biddlesworth. She made no comment at all to me which I found rather surprising. And indeed, when I asked for one she was remarkably short with me. I was quite pleased that I was going to England by myself.

By the end of 1866 I was installed in a house in Anglesea Road Surbiton where I had been advised many of my colleagues had found similar houses to pass their English furloughs. It took some arranging for I had to do everything myself, including all those matters that someone in my station would normally leave to their wives. I think that it is fair to say that 1866 was the most important year in my life. After that year everything changed for me and...but you can agree with me or no as you wish, once you have read the remainder of what I have here set down. I must aver though that 1866 was for me pivotal year.

It began with me attending the wedding of Jack Whicher to his erstwhile landlady, Charlotte Piper, on 21st August in St Margaret's which is a small church situated within the grounds of Westminster Abbey. You will remember that I had met Jack in 1862 when I had come over to the wedding of his niece, Sarah to that gallant fellow who so deservedly was awarded the Victoria Cross. At that time Jack made it plain to me that he knew something of my work. Now, after his wedding to a lady three years his senior, he insisted that were I ever to need assistance I should not hesitate to call upon him to supply it. I promised him that I would remember his offer. He told me that he had now retired, and being comfortably off, as his pension was more than adequate now that he had married, he liked to work as a private investigator.

You must not imagine that throughout my career I kept my nose permanently to the grindstone. I frequently sought diversions of various kinds, including on one occasion going to the opera. Well that may have surprised you, but it will not be a surprise to you to hear that the opera that I chose to honour with my attention dealt with war. It was, of course: "La Fille du Regiment". What a ridiculous plot, and what unbelievable characters. But as it was so very far from the truth of army life it was amusing. My charming companion who was with me that night indicated that that was probably the intention of the people who wrote the opera to do exactly that: amuse me. I was certainly entertained and never more so when the hero sang: 'Ah! mes amis, quel jour de fête!' Those incredible top Cs! We both applauded enthusiastically. Even at this time I am unable to divulge just who it was that joined me in that applause and subsequently in a late champagne supper. Some things are better never revealed. I can reveal however that I stuck to the music hall ever after that for entertainment.

PART TWO

1866, A Momentous Year for Me

Chapter 13

1866

A stone in the shoe, a bug in the ear, a speck of dust in the eye, a thorn in the foot, and a quarrel in the family, however small in themselves, are unspeakably tormenting.

I sighed in satisfaction as I sat down at last in a chair and lit a cheroot. I hoped that I had brought enough of them from India to last me through my leave. I tried to push that thought away as I knew that i had more important matters with which to occupy my mind. I had been charged with some delicate negotiations while I was here and I had been told to keep my wits about me. I was disturbed by a scream from below that was followed by a red-faced parlour maid at the door, her red face matching her hair that was in danger of tumbling down, caused by her hurried rush upstairs.

"What now?"

"Please. Cook says that she cannot work with those heathens in her kitchen."

This time my sigh was one of exasperation. I carefully stubbed out my cheroot and said:

"Tell her...No wait, I'll come myself."

As I followed Maureen O'Grady downstairs into a much less well-furnished part of the house I wondered whether my wife who was back in India would have made a better job of renting this house in Anglesea Road and recruiting the staff. It was really far bigger than I needed, but I had been persuaded to take it as the rent had been so low. I had brought only two servants with me, Raj Dal and Mamoud Patel. I had been warned that bringing my Indian servants with me to England would not be a good idea. I had ignored the warnings for both Raj Dal and Mamoud Patel had been such staunch supporters in my work to deal with Thuggee and dacoits that I felt that they were almost an extension of myself. It had surprised others in India when I had both a Moslem and a Sikh working together so closely with me, but I had persevered with them for they were both extremely talented. My apparent ignoring of their different religious beliefs had been deliberate and did not spring from an ignorance of those beliefs. In fact I had studied what Moslems and Sikh's believed. I had read their holy books and discussed them at some depth earning their respect as a result.

Naturally in India I had other servants. In fact I had servants who took care of hiring servants. Here in England I had left it to an agency that had sent me a cook who seemed unable to accept the idea that Indian servants should also be employed in the household. I was finally able to make some sort of peace, only to be interrupted by the maid who announced that someone had come to be interviewed for the post of housekeeper. I told the maid to send the women up to the room that he was presently using and that I would see her there.

I had only just reached the first floor room when the maid showed in a youngish woman dressed soberly and carrying a large wet umbrella, that Maureen should have taken from her. Without another word a stony-faced Maureen went out and shut the door. The woman handed an envelope to me that contained her character. I opened it and perused its contents. Meanwhile the closed umbrella dripped onto the carpet ignored by me, so the young woman furled it and put it into the empty grate where a little pool of water grew as I read her character that was quite satisfactory I was pleased to note.

The woman who stood before me showed in her stance a certain defiance that I found disturbing. I was unsettled by it for I normally found women to be meek, submissive, obedient creatures as indeed they should be, and certainly never defiant. Even Caroline when I taxed her with her lapse had simply agreed that she had been in the wrong.

"You are?" I asked.

"I am Mrs Bollen. You will have seen my name on the papers that I have given you."

There was a hint of pertness in this answer that I chose to ignore.

"Should you be seeking employment as a married woman? Your husband..."

"Is dead. I am a widow."

"Ah!"

My mind went back to India and the procession that I had watched that had been meant to end in the immolation of an Indian widow. I had saved her only to find that her relatives took her back, then removed her to a village where she became suttee by her own hands. The popular image of the victim of suttee is of a beautiful Indian maiden who is forced against her will to a despicable act. The real truth is that the widow is often old and ugly and quite ready to join her husband and to cease to be a burden on her relatives. In any case, in India death is not seen in the same way as we regard it...

"Mr Driscoll?"

Brought back to the present by the sharp use of my name, I left India refocused my eyes and said:

"I am so sorry Mrs Bollen. Do please excuse me. I was thinking of..."

I paused. Mrs Bollen cocked her head sideways like a bright-eyed robin inspecting a grub.

"Yes?"

I smiled at her, sure that this widow in Surbiton would not be interested in my memories of the suttee of another widow in a far-away country and probably totally unable to understand the complexities of other cultures anyway.

"Well, never mind what I was thinking of. I see that you have a good character."

I paused and this gave Mrs Bollen the opportunity to ask me a question.

"Please do not think me impertinent but should I not be interviewed by your wife sir?"

"Normally you would be", I replied somewhat stiffly, "but she is still in India and I do need a housekeeper."

Even as I said this the door was opened by Maureen O'Grady who said immediately over the loud banging and clattering that accompanied her entry:

"Please sir, it's Cook. She wants to know..."

My look was enough to stop her in her tracks. She backed out and could be heard sobbing outside the room.

"Mrs Bollen. You see how it is."

"I do indeed."

She waited. Maureen was now wailing.

"Please Mrs Bollen. Could you please take the post of housekeeper immediately? I would be most obligated to you; we can discuss terms in due course."

Mrs Bollen smiled and curtsied, and nodding her agreement left the room smartly, where after a sharp word and a murmured conversation she took the housemaid downstairs. In due course a passable meal was served in the dining room and afterwards Mrs Bollen, now divested of her coat, but still dressed soberly, came back.

"If you please I should like to go now and collect my things so that I can return and take up my duties correctly. I trust that your meal was satisfactory? As you might expect I have spoken to Cook and Maureen, who by the way is really quite a good maid, and only needs firm directing. I have also made the acquaintance of both your Indian servants and I am sure that we shall all be able to run your household much as you would expect."

"Thank you Mrs Bollen. Do please act as you suggest. Shall we discuss terms to morrow?"

"That will be quite acceptable."

It was only when she had left the room that I remembered her umbrella that was still in the grate. For a moment I considered going after her with it thinking to overtake her and return it. I resisted the thought. How unseemly that would be I told myself.

The following day the morning post comprised one letter only. The letter simply said that I was to go to Windsor and gave an address where I would be expected. Pleased to be rid of the house and its women I set off early. The trains were on time and I was soon there. The address turned out to be a plain looking house where I banged on the door and was received by a burly doorman who looked remarkably similar to a soldier. He looked at my letter and said:

"The colonel is expecting you."

I was shown upstairs immediately into a snug study where a much younger man than I had expected to see greeted me. He wasted no time in explaining what was afoot.

"You see Driscoll, the whole purpose of this exercise is to change the feelings that exist about Indian Moslems. Ever since our debacles in Afghanistan and the mutiny there has been bad feelings here in England over the members of that religion. To that end we want you to find us a suitable young Moslem Indian who can be introduced into the Queen's household. He has to be a suitable chap whose behaviour must be that of a paragon. It's a daring plan for we want him to influence the Queen; we know that she is likely to be influenced by him for she has manifested an interest in all things Indian. If she indicates a positive attitude towards this man it could set the whole tone for the future. I won't beat about the bush with you as I expect you will already be ahead of me. The fact of the matter is the Prime Minister is worried about India and Russia. There, I've said it. You probably guessed where all this was going anyway."

"Well sir, setting aside the purpose, how can you be sure that the Queen is really interested enough to make this work?"

Well, we know that when that chappie Meadows Taylor was writing about the Thugs in his book, what was it called?"

"Confessions of a Thug."

"Yes, that's the one. Lot of balderdash of course; she was so damn impatient to read the next chapter that she sent out to have it rushed to her so that she could read it before it was published. She was, and still is fascinated with the way that Thuggee was and is being dealt with. That's the reason why we have chosen you to be the major person in this enterprise; we know that you have had some successes and are well regarded in some quarters."

127

He tapped with his pipe the file of papers that were on his desk, smiling as he did so.

"If we are successful we shall secure Afghanistan as an ally for all time. Just think. No more fighting. This could be a truly permanent Moslem entente cordiale. It could last for ever."

"For ever?"

"Look, there is nothing, but nothing so powerful as religion. If we can send out a message about the way we regard Islam it will override all those tribal factions. Remember, Islam is the religion of peace and it is also the religion of Afghanistan so we shall have allied ourselves to something more powerful than people."

He tapped his papers again.

"Everyone has a file you know. And by the by, we also know about 'you know who' who has been such a trouble to you."

Now he tapped his nose with the stem of his pipe as he went on:

" We have had our eye on him for a while. He seems to be able to meet his mess bills and gaming debts with remarkable ease. It would not surprise us to discover that they are met from funds other than the ones that he keeps at Coutts."

There was a pause; the fire crackled and the clock ticked. I broke the silence.

"So what exactly do you require of me?"

"It's all in here", he said pushing a fat envelope towards me.

"Its all quite clearly set out in this document. Once you have read it you will know what our wishes are; how you do it will depend upon you of course. Do not rush. This is a long term strategy that we want to put in place."

Leaving the warm room and comfortable house I wrapped my coat around me and set off. Behind me I heard footsteps. Thinking that someone was hurrying after me with some extra papers or something that I had forgotten I turned around and so saved my life. The cloth that was whirled around my neck only caught me on the side and my assailant was not able to put his knee in my back and pull it back to strangle me. I kicked back at him. He grunted. He let go. He pulled at my bag. And as I would not let it go he pulled me into the mud where my hat rolled off into the dirty gutter. Before I could even cry out he was gone and so had my bag. I tried to get up but found that I was shaking. My legs would not support me.

I was helped to my feet, and the scarf around my neck was unwound. I took it and gestured to my hat. It was recovered and given to me. I recognised the burly man who handed it back to me as the man who had both let me in and seen me out.

"I was to follow you to make sure that you were safe. I'm sorry. I seemed to have been too late."

I looked into my hat. I ignored the mud. The papers were still there, thank God.

"Not at all. Not at all. It seems that they have shown their hand, whoever they are."

I undid the knot at the corner of the scarf and took out the rupee that was in it. I held it out to the doorman as I got into the cab. I leaned out to do so.

"Give this to the Colonel will you please with my compliments."

He hesitated so I raised my voice.

"It's not a tip man, it's a hint."

He nodded at that, took the rupee and indicated to the driver that he should go.

I recognised the scarf which I now carefully folded and put into my pocket as the cab trundled off. It was a rumal, the cloth traditionally used by thugs to strangle their victims. I might need it as evidence. I own I was shaken. I had experienced trouble in India but never had anyone tried to kill me in this fashion, and in the open in Windsor! 'Those blackguards must either be thugs or have learned their technique from thugs', I thought.

I pulled my collar up to hide my bruised neck, wincing as I did so. It would never do to arrive home in this state. I decided to stay in the club in town where I was an honorary member. However as I went into the foyer, where the doorman luckily remembered me, a hearty clap on my back made me groan for I just knew that it would be that Irish writer who had been having such success with his plays, and as a consequence thought that everyone wanted to know him.

I actually loathed him, disliking his flamboyance and, although I owned that he was indeed clever, I knew just how contrived were his 'bon mots'. Someone, I can't remember who, told me that he worked on them, and even stole them and passed them off as his own.

"My dear chap, how remarkable that I should see you here. A little bird told me that you were in Windsor. I said to myself that you must have gone there to see the Queen. There's no other possible reason to go to that dreary dreary town, although some would say that having to have a conversation with her Majesty can be equally dreary. Now, I don't know if you have met my friend. May I introduce..."

Incensed by his words and not at all impressed by the languid drooping youth who accompanied him, I cut him short, saying that I was sorry but I was fatigued and wished to retire early.

Chapter 14

1866

Danger should be feared when distant, and braved when present

After my overnight stay at the club I was appalled at the livid reddish purple mark on my neck that I saw when I shaved in the morning. I dressed, pulled my neckpiece up as far as possible and went out to get some salve. I realised that the playwright must have glimpsed the bruising on my neck and had spoken to someone because as soon as I reached the foyer I was approached by Forbes-Bosely who grinned and said:

"I hope your neck is better. I didn't know you liked them rough old chap!"

I told him to go to the devil and looked for a chemist shop. When I came out into the street I saw Forbes-Bosely out of the corner of my eye. He was holding an umbrella and talking to someone, a young woman that I thought I knew, who also carried an umbrella; but before I could get a good look at them he had turned away. As he did so he pointed at me and nodded. She said something to him and he nodded again. She bobbed a sketchy curtsey and left him to push herself through the crowds towards me. I was suspicious. I tried to move away but the crowd was too thick.

"Have a care sir", someone said angrily as I forced on, so I was perforce obliged to desist. Because she was so small she slid through the throng like an eel and ended up at my side as I was moved along in the crush.

"Sir", she said.

I tried to ignore her, but she plucked at my sleeve with one hand as she grasped her umbrella firmly with the other and would not be shaken off. Eventually I turned to her and saw a pretty face marred by a slightly overfull mouth that was balanced by excessively brown eyes the colour of toffee, all surrounded by one of those bonnets that women seem to consider to be so important.

"Go away" I said rudely.

The toffee-coloured eyes filled with tears. I nearly succumbed to the lachrymose blackmail but fought against sentiment and exclaimed even more rudely:

"I said go away. Leave me be."

"Mrs Bollen sent me."

I stopped short causing a lady to cannon into me. I apologised to her. Her slight bow of acceptance was accompanied by a withering glance at my bad manners. I turned to my little tormenter saying:

"Foolish child. Why did you not say so immediately."

Quite overlooking the fact that I had scarcely given her the opportunity to do so.

"She sent me to say that you had better hurry home. I am her daughter sir."

I had not realised that Mrs Bollen had a daughter but I might have seen in those peculiar coloured eyes the same determination that I had already perceived in Mrs Bollen's clear gaze. That was why I thought that I had recognised her.

"Why?"

"Why what sir?"

Fighting back impatience I said:

"Why does she say that I should come home?"

She looked down, traced a figure in the dirt with her umbrella and said nothing. I afterwards learned that it had been absolute torture for her to even approach me with a message for she was so shy a youngster. In fact she was unable to give me a reason for her message to me had been simply that it were best for me to return quickly to Surbiton. Trusting to Mrs Bollen's good judgement we hurried together towards the terminus where we boarded a train. My neckerchief was pulled up as far as I could get it in order to hide the livid red mark upon my neck that was all the remained of the attack upon me. We still attracted attention however.

Mrs Bollen saw the mark immediately as I entered my household. Nothing escaped her.

"Thank God that you are safe."

"Why should I not be? Why did you send your daughter to fetch me?"

She ignored my questions and said instead:

"Go home now Amelia. You have done well."

Turning to me as Amelia said obediently:

"Yes mama." and left, she added:

"There's been another…" she hesitated.

"Another?"

"Another death."

She hurried on lifting a hand to forestall any question that I might put.

"They say that it was a train accident."

"Who says?"

She brushed aside my question, saying:

"But I hear that he was strangled."

My hand went of its own accord to my neck and Mrs Bollen smiled grimly.

"Tell me all you know." I said.

"I shall, but first let me tell cook that you are returned and desirous of taking some food. I expect that you are hungry are you not?"

It was my turn to ignore a question. I was eager to hear everything that she could tell me.

"It's another death on the railway just like my husband's death. A railway worker who they are saying has had an accident; but why I wish to know has he strangle marks on his neck, and why is there to be no inquest?"

"How did you hear about this, and how did you get the details?"

"I still have friends whose husbands work on the railway. One of them told me about it. She overheard the ganger telling her husband not to say anything to anyone. When she made a fuss they threatened to call the police, so for the sake of her husband keeping his employment she agreed to keep quiet then came to tell me for she knew that I had lost my husband in similar circumstances."

By now I was sure that we ought to inform the police as the attack upon myself and that upon another railway worker of a similar nature indicated to my way of thinking that there was some kind of conspiracy or plot afoot. I then remembered Jack Whicher, so I not only sent a message to the constabulary but also a telegram to Jack. Having done this we settled down to await their arrival.

Mrs Bollen, I realised was no ordinary women so I asked her to tell of her early years. At first she exhibited a certain natural reluctance so I pressed her and she gave in to my request to hear her history.

"I am the only daughter of parents who were originally employed on the land. When the factories came to be built they moved from the land into a town, Redditch, where they were employed in the making of needles and similar articles. It was boring repetitive work but it kept a roof over their heads. I say that I am the only daughter, but my mother had several children, losing them all at an early age. They decided that they had to escape such a place that killed children soon after they entered this world, so they came to London where they both found employment in a large house as servants.

When I was born they used a small amount of money to start a dairy. I cannot tell you where the money originated. I think that it came from the lady of the house where they were employed who was widowed and wanted to assist some of her old servants. The dairy prospered until one day when my father fell down in the street as he was going about his rounds and was pronounced dead. Soon after my mother simply withered away. It began as a lump in her chest. It was obviously more than that as my husband and I observed. She simply seemed to give up all hope. Following her death I went into service like so many young women did. Then I met my late husband who took me away from that life.

I had married young and was blessed with Amelia who you have met. She is a sweet natured child, industrious and willing, and now that her father is dead is a prop and comfort to me for I could never marry again. My husband worked upon the railway that pushed its tentacles from the centre of that grimy smoky disease-ridden stinking thing that men call London. I have heard that it is held up to the world as a model of what cities ought to be; expanding, lively, forward looking and proving to be everything that anybody could desire. I have another opinion that is not so flattering. I think that everything that is dirty, vicious, immoral, degraded and disgusting can be had in London; and the taking of such things degrades many of its inhabitants no how high or lowly their state. I think I shock you with my violent views?"

I said nothing. I was shocked. Not at her views but at her ability to express them. In my experience women are usually only able to comment in the most vapid way about such matters as bonnets or garments of some sort. Wha kind of woman had I taken under my roof? I think that she took my shocked silence for agreement for she went on:

"Luckily we were able to move to Surbiton where at the outskirts we found a cottage at a modest rent and my husband could continue his employment on the railway. The hours were long and it was dangerous work, but, thank God, he was in continuous employment. It was not always possible for him to attend church on a Sunday because of his railway duties so we had to pray on his behalf when we went, not that our prayers were heeded for he was taken from us.

There is something strange about his death. It was held to be an accident and the railway were content to accept that verdict, but Charlie Freeman, who was there, told me that there was a red mark on my husband's neck. He told me that it for all the world as if my husband had been strangled."

Having heard her out I wanted to think about what she had told me, so to buy some time I commented upon her daughter and said how pleasant it must be to have a child such as she. She repeated that Amelia was indeed a great comfort to her, but asked did I not have a child myself? Raj Dal had mentioned to her that I was a father. My look stopped her in half-sentence. Any other woman might have blundered on but she waited calmly for me to gain some of my composure then said quietly:

"Tell me if I am wrong, but do I sense that you are troubled in this matter?"

I nodded too full of unspoken emotions to give it words. She waited.

"Perhaps I should withdraw and leave you to gather yourself together?"

"No, not at all, do please stay. It would be a great comfort and relief to me to tell someone about this."

Chapter 15

1866

Without a true friend a man cannot discern the nature of his own actions

"Tell me then what happened."

"I had been away. Not unusual for me. I often went to some outlying station, but I must admit that I wanted to get away; after all having babies is women's business is it not?

Mrs Bollen smiled encouragingly but did not answer.

"Right. So I had been away, and before I went the cantonment doctor had assured me that everything was fine with Caroline. Over cigars and brandy I told him that we had hired an amah who came highly recommended, and I had been impressed with her too when I saw her. You must realise that we had over thirty servants, and my major domo would organise them to make sure that my household ran smoothly. Just as you indeed keep this establishment going like clockwork."

Mrs Bollen rearranged her hands and gave a slight nod in recognition of the compliment.

"So you see I was not expecting the long faces that I saw as I rode in, dusty, muddy, sweating and smelling of horses and leather. I wanted a bath and a chota peg, not bad news. I braced myself and went straight into Caroline pushing past the amah who said that I should wait. She was sitting up in bed looking pale and apprehensive. I kissed her as the baby was brought to me. I was about to ask was it a boy. I wanted a boy, for the first you know, when I realised why everyone was looking glum. Now you have seen my hair. It's red. Caroline's is fair, sort of gold. I could not have paler skin with freckles and my wife's skin, unless she imprudently allows the sun to touch it, is parchment white.

If I do not wear a helmet in India my face can get as red as my hair. My wife's eyes are blue; mine are hazel. I tell you this so that you can imagine my feelings when the child that I was shown had dark skin and brown hair. There could be no doubt that this child was not mine."

Mrs Bollen looked at me. She took my hand.

"Things may not be as you think."

I found her hand on mine immensely comforting and I made no move to withdraw it, despite the fact that for a servant as she was it was not something that I ought to allow. I recognised however that as a woman she would have derived some satisfaction from offering such comfort, so I permitted her to indulge herself. We sat like this for several seconds and only drew apart when the maid came in with a letter. It was from Caroline who told me amongst other matters that her childhood friend was in London and would be calling upon me. I had never met Elizabet de Groot, but Caroline had often spoken of her in the warmest possible terms, saying how sensible she was. Days later Elizabet did indeed call and I must set out what she said. In the meantime I continued to wait for the police and for Jack Whicher.

143

Effie, looking pink, came in to say that an Inspector had called. Pleased that I had such a quick response I told Effie to show him up immediately.

The inspector was polite but dismissive. Yes, there had been a death, but no, he could not let Mr Driscoll see the body. He was waiting himself to see the results of the autopsy. A Dr Black-Heaton was at this very moment carrying this out.

"Well, I suppose that his findings will be available at the inquest", I observed mildly looking at the inspector as I did so.

The inspector looked uncomfortable.

"In point of fact", he began, "Actually", he continued, his colour now slightly pinker than it had been earlier when he had been glacially dismissive of my interest, "Well to tell the truth."

He paused, obviously seeking a turn of phrase that would explain what he really could not reveal.

"The facts of the matter are such that…"

"…you have been instructed to keep this matter out of sight", I said quietly.

"Well not exactly 'instructed', but certain intimations have been received by those in authority that mean it is incumbent upon us to…"

"…keep the whole matter quiet", said Mrs Bollen acidly.

The inspector's respectful attitude towards me, a gentleman, was not manifest now that an underling, and a woman at that, had seen fit to intervene. He turned to her, shook his head at her lack of understanding, and despite his now high colour in his cheeks that revealed his feelings said:

"We, that is to say the good offices of Scotland Yard have this matter well in hand, and I can tell you that the decision to treat this situation with the utmost discretion has been taken as a matter of the highest priority, the very highest priority."

He was about to add more when Effie came in to announce that a Mr Whicher was at the front door and should she show him up please? She showed in her manner and high colour the extreme excitement that two such sensational visitors had thrown the household into. Ignoring her excitement, I told Effie that she should indeed show up Mr Whicher immediately. In the ensuing pause the inspector's colour returned to normal and he smiled confidently. His confidence however was somewhat shaken when Mr Whicher, hat in hand as he had been in such a hurry to come upstairs, came into the room, crossed it to shake my hand warmly, saying as he did so:

"My dear Manfred. I got your telegram and came at once."

Chapter 16

1866

Wisdom assists more than strength.

Once the inspector had got over the shock that it was not he whom Whicher had come to see but me, we got on famously. The inspector was even able to accept that a servant might be allowed to join in on our deliberations. I accordingly arranged for Nicola to order tea for everyone and told her to sit with us as we deliberated. Now that Whicher had joined our party it became mysteriously possible for the inspector to tell us the whole story, and he proceeded to do so. We listened and when Nicola at one point was about to interrupt I gave her a warning look. The inspector finished by saying:

"So you see. It's very clear that these men were killed by their own negligence. A common occurrence.

In the silence that followed he added:

"Unfortunately."

I said:

"No, not so. Everything points to the fact that these man were dead before the wagon hit him. If he had been examined properly it would have been manifestly clear that that his neck had been broken before the apparent accident."

"That's ridiculous. How could his neck have been broken as you describe? Why do you think this is happening?"

I looked at the inspector steadily. I knew that he had been told to hush up these deaths. What would he say to my explanation?

I spoke quietly:

"It could have been done by a man... it resembles those deaths that I remember in India. It reminds me of what Sleeman discovered and what I thought we had got rid of. As to why I think it is happening, it is still difficult to judge. But let us look at the facts."

Whicher nodded.

"Yes, let's have the facts."

I ticked them off on my fingers.

"One: someone or some persons are killing people using the methods of thuggee here in England, in Surbiton. Two: with one exception, the murders are all carried out on the railway. Three: the authorities seem keen to go along with the idea that the murders are accidents. Now I must turn to conjecture. It seems to be about religion for we believe that somehow the Goddess Kali, the Great destroyer, might be involved.

"How can a Goddess be a destroyer? Surely she should be protecting life should she not?"

"Do remember that we all have to die and that everything and everybody is reborn in some way. Perhaps the Goddess Kali simply reminds us how everything has to be destroyed in order that more can live."

We decided that as the police were now completely alerted to the dangers we could safely leave it to them. I was warned not to leave the house for the next few days and agreed that, irksome as this bar to my freedom would be, I would bear with it.

When the maid had show the inspector and Jack Whicher out I said to Mrs Bollen:

"Mrs Bollen, Nicola, I am told that there is a studio nearby where one might have one's likenesses taken. I understand that several people have intimated that the result is extremely good and they were quite delighted with the portraits that were produced. It would give me the greatest pleasure were you to go to this establishment and obtain a portrait of yourself."

"What would be the purpose of this?"

"The purpose would be to furnish me with a reminder of a servant who I have come to rely upon and who..."

I faltered. The look that Nicola was giving me made me pause. I realised that Nicola had come to represent much more to me than a mere servant and that she had discerned this fact. I said boldly:

"Nicola, you..."

I stopped. She waited, something that she excelled in. I cleared my throat but before I could say anything she said:

"Of course I shall have my likeness taken, and when I give it to you I shall expect you to receive it in the very same spirit that I shall give it to you. And do remember that there is no fool quite like an old fool."

I was about the ask her to elaborate upon this gnomic statement of hers when Amelia entered the room. She, having heard the end of her mother's statement and seeing my face and her mother's, said as she gathered together some materials:

"I think that I had better go now. I will await you at home. I have this sewing that I should attend to. Why Mama, have you a fever? You look quite flushed!"

Nicola reassured her daughter about her state of health and sent her home. We then sat together in front of the fire once she had departed and I decided that I should not, could not ask her to say anything more. After a while she excused herself to return to her duties and I read the newspaper.

It became very late in the evening and quite dark. The weather was normal; that is to say that it was raining again. I was idly watching the wet shrubbery that was lit from the lights in the front room, having exhausted what news interested me in the Times when Mrs Bollen came in to say that she needed to go home. I followed her out to the hallway where she looked for her umbrella. She could not see it anywhere so I called the maid and she looked too. Still no sign of it so I said:

"Take mine", and opened the front door.

The rain had increased. The wind had too. It was a really nasty night.

"Better wait."

"I cannot. Amelia is waiting for me. I thank you for your offer of the umbrella but I fear it will be too large. It will blow away and possibly take me with it. We are but poor feeble women you know."

This last comment was accompanied by her trying to put on one of those ridiculous bonnets that did nothing to protect women from the elements. I knew that she was mocking me so I took my hat from the hat stand, took away her bonnet and gave my hat to her with a deep bow.

"Then put this on. It will at least keep your hair dry. She accepted it with a mock curtsey smiling as she did so. The maid, who was watching this exchange, was sent packing by Mrs Bollen glaring at her, but I could help but see that the maid went off downstairs with a smile.

I held the door against the wind and Mrs Bollen turned to thank me. She turned her face up to me, I suppose to say goodbye, and impulsively I kissed her. Yes, I know that it was wrong of me. I also know it was foolish, and the moment I did it both those thoughts came to me. But imagine my surprise when instead of drawing away in shock or anger or disgust, she kissed me back!

Chapter 17

1866

The relations of all living end in separation. They arise and they disappear, like bubbles upon the water

I watched her go out of sight then went back inside. I returned to my warm comfortable room and sat down. What had I done? I had let myself be led astray that's what I had done. But why had I done so, I asked myself? I went over carefully what she had told me. From that I was led into considering her intelligence, and from that the excitement that I always felt when discussing any matter with her. Why, she was almost like a man in the way that she considered facts and discussed them. That was it! I admired her because of her mind that I thought might nearly be equal to mine. I firmly pushed away any thoughts to do with her body. Of course she was an attractive woman, but only a servant...My thoughts were interrupted by a frantic knocking on he front door.

The maid showed in a bedraggled Amelia whose red eyes showed that she had been crying. If there were any doubt about that fact she started to cry in dreadful sobs again while the maid looked on wide-eyed.

"Whatever is it Amelia?"

"She's dead. They have taken her to the morgue. I am to tell you to come there straightaway."

I knew better than to ask who she was talking about. Only the death of her mother could cause such an outburst of grief. I heard a cry. It was the maid.

"Oh no. Not Mrs Bollen."

At the morgue I looked down at her pathetic broken body and felt such a surge of emotion such as I had never ever felt before. This surprised me as I had seen so many bodies in my time, none of which had ever before moved me in this fashion. I thought about it as I went back to my strangely quiet house. My emotion was not simply that of regret at her death, but also guilt. Why did I feel such guilt? It was partly that it seems that as she was wearing my hat she might have been mistaken for me so I may have therefore been the cause of he death. It was more than that though; along with that guilt was another guilty feeling that we ought never to have kissed. Why, I asked myself did I let myself be tempted by her?

With the police on the alert, the assailant had been caught as he tried to escape. I was told that almost as soon as he had been arrested he had confessed. It was clear that he had mistaken Mrs Bollen for myself and that he had been sent from India to assassinate me. I was apparently seen as a threat to those who wished India to be run by Indians. I thought to myself as I heard this, how stupid they were think that they could turn the clock back to the glory days of the Mughals. But why had he murdered the railway men? And why try to cover it up?

The answer was both less and more complicated than I had supposed it would be, and it was all to do with Thomas Brassey. Thomas Brassey had lived for a while in Surbiton and was to all the world the successful railway engineer. Indeed as I have already said I had been in the past involved in getting him to provide India with trains. This slight acquaintance was sufficient for the assassin to imagine that there was a connection between us. The deaths on the railway were a warning to Brassey. He was supposed to take note of these warnings and cease his activities. That was the less complicated part.

The more complicated part was that, unknown to me, Thomas Brassey had been recruited in London to send back any information that he might come across in his work. He had been recruited by the same organisation that I had visited in 1862 soon after the Russian war. They had seen in him a patriot who would assist the country of his birth and he had agreed to be of assistance. He travelled widely and wrote all his own correspondence, sometimes staying up late into the night to do so. He would pass on what he heard or saw. As an example, he might, in concluding a contact, find out that others were also buying large quantities of steel. This fact by itself meant nothing, but when added to all the other small pieces of information available to London office it might take on a greater significance.

Incidentally the assailant revealed that his paymasters hailed from Yalta. He also confessed that he had been contracted to remove me but only to scare off Thomas Brassey. Brassey's death would have caused too much fuss. I, on the other hand was considered to be of much less importance, so my death, whilst useful, would have hardly attracted a newspaper headline. In any case, I knew that my demise would have been quietly dealt with just as they were going to deal with Mrs Bollen's.

Amelia sought me out the following day. I had always found her to be quiet and withdrawn. She had changed overnight. I was sure that the death of her father and now her mother had affected her badly for she poured out her thoughts to me in a torrent of words that I could scarcely keep up with. Eventually she fell silent. How cruel life could be. I resolved to use what influence I had to assist Amelia.

I was brought back to my own life by a visitor. It was Elizabet de Groot. I was shocked to find that she travelled by herself in the train to Surbiton, and laughed at what she declared were my old fashioned ideas about women. It felt wrong somehow to be alone with her in my drawing room and I took care to seat myself across the room so that were a servant to see us there could be no mistaking our relationship. I was alarmed however when she asked me bluntly about my son. Surely I thought Caroline has not been so imprudent to confide in her old friend the circumstances surrounding his birth?

Women are such volatile creatures. I suspected that despite all that I had said to Caroline when I assured her that I had made such adequate arrangements for the boy and sworn her to silence she had told Elizabet de Groot all. I was proved right for Elizabet de Groot immediately confronted me telling me that I was wrong about the boy's father.

"Oh! you foolish man. Your Caroline came to India from Holland did she not?"

"Yes, from Utrecht. I was enchanted by her delicate pale pink Dutch skin and blue eyes that went so well with her delicate complexion that made her seem so doll-like."

"But did you never consider her parents? Did you never think where they came from?"

"Holland, I supposed", I said.

156

"God give me strength", said Elizabet, then went on:

"Caroline's maiden name was Hoostracht and her grandparents were living in Goa before they came back to Holland. If you had asked them you would have been told that Caroline's grandfather Jan Steen went to Goa to make his fortune and while he was there he married an Indian lady that he always averred was a princess. When he came back he brought his wife with him, unlike many I might add. In fact she came from a high caste Brahmin family who disowned her when she married a European for love.

In time they had three children who survived. In fact she had seven in all, but three did not survive beyond the first year and another was carried off by cholera. Actually this was the principal reason that Caroline's grandparents came to Holland; the other main reason was the fact that Jan Steen Boorviegen had made a fortune from trading and wanted to come home. With these riches at his command the good burghers of Utrecht were more than willing to overlook Caroline's grandmother's dusky complexion, particularly as she was a pious lady who always attended the church and gave readily to charity.

Their second child was christened Maria Christine Caroline de Boorviegen and when she was old enough she was married to Pieter Hoostracht who turned out to be much less successful as an artist than everyone hoped. Your Caroline was their second child. So you see that your wife has had a child who has inherited his looks from his grandmother, which is not so very unusual. Farmers have always known about such matters. It is called a throwback. Your wife has therefore not been unfaithful to you; rather, I should say, it is you who have been insensitive and stupid."

157

If Elizabet de Groot had slapped me in the face, I could not have been more shocked. That someone could accuse me to my face of being stupid! I sat still then said coldly:

"That's all well and good. I grant that you may very well be right in your assertions, but I shall require more proof than your word on this matter."

Once again I was to be shocked. This impertinent woman replied:

"Oh! you and your proof. You are not in India now bringing poor peasants into court and browbeating them into making admissions of guilt."

Stung by what I considered to be a slanderous attack upon my name and methods, I, who had been about to concede that I ought in fact to my wife's family history so that I could forgive her, resumed my former cold tone of voice and said:

"You forget yourself. You are speaking of matters that do not concern you; and in any case you can have no real understanding of them."

I turned away, sure I had finished this less than desirable conversation with this so-called friend of my wife, only to be astonished when she said impudently:

"Do I not? Tell me Manfred Driscoll just how you as an Englishman came to be called Manfred rather than George or Arthur or..."

My reddening cheeks stopped Elizabet from going on. She had hit a tender spot.

I remembered my first day at school when I had been obliged to defend my Christian name. Challenged by the other boys to explain my 'foreign' name I had mistakenly decided to fight my chief tormentor - and lost. To add to my troubles, I was then beaten by an under master for brawling and ungentlemanly behaviour. As a consequence I formed a group of boys who were 'different' in some way. In my case it was my grandfather came from Bavaria, and because I was bi-lingual, German being spoken at home as often as English. I was not only bi-lingual but a quick learner of languages I became a favourite of some masters who defended our group to some extent. I was to find that his swift mastery of languages was most useful in India.

I looked at Elizabet. She was right. Perhaps I ought to give my wife the benefit of the doubt in this matter. I cleared my throat.

"I'm sorry. You are correct in practically all respects. I do have reason than most to concede this."

"Well, I never ever thought that I would hear an apology from you Manfred", said Elizabet, then added quickly before I could say anything:

"All I ask is that you check the records to see that all that I have told you is the truth."

With this Parthian shot Elizabet left me to ponder her revelations.

Faced with what Elizabet had told me so forcefully I was still unwilling to look for documentary proof of what she had said. I decided instead that I would do nothing about the boy but would reinstate my wife in my affections. This partially helped to assuage the guilty feelings that I had experienced about the relationship that I had had with Mrs Bollen.

I told myself however that I had needed to maintain that relationship that was warmer and more intimate than was usual between a master and servant. I felt that I had needed it so that I could continue that struggle against something that so puzzled me; I had taken this decision because, she had proved such an ally in that endeavour. At the back of my mind lurked the thought that I was trying to rationalise my behaviour. I ignored it as best as I was able and turned to think about my return to India. For it was time that I returned there.

Before I left I contacted General Dennehy who was my contact in the palace and I asked him for a favour. As a result he was instrumental in ensuring that Amelia was given a place in the royal household in Osborne House. She was employed as a servant at terms that were most generous considering her lack of experience. I felt that it was the very least that I could do to assist her, and in any case it would be useful to have her there. I asked her to write to me saying that I would be most interested in any thing she had to tell me. I was right on both counts. She looked on me as someone who respected her mother and her mother's opinions, and in time, as a result came to regard me almost as a father. Certainly I felt more for her than I would normally have felt for a mere servant's daughter.

As to her usefulness, she was a naive young woman who had been well brought up by her mother and as a consequence could write a fair hand, but her grammar was not always as good as it might be, something that I was prepared to overlook. What was more she had an eye for detail that rivalled my own. Her letters to me were filled with what went on in the royal household in Osborne House, and later on what she observed in the other royal establishments for she worked in Windsor Castle as well as Balmoral. I must say here that I never at any time indicated my concern at what she wrote, useful as it was to me; instead I simply responded as a father would to her fulsome letters and as a result gained a complete picture of what went on in those establishments.

I know that what I was getting was from a lowly servants point of view. Now you might imagine that such accounts would have no value, and that is where you would be totally mistaken. It is so astonishing what is said in front of servants. Employers seem to think that because they stand there silently that they are taking no more notice than the walls. It used to be said 'if only walls could speak'. Well this young woman told me a great deal over the years, I can tell you! So my story from now on relies as much upon her letters to me as my own observations.

The following small excerpt is an example of the sort of detail that she sent me. It included a whole lot of trivia on what the staff were supposed to wear etc.

"When I was being instructed in how to address various persinages I was told the following story. The Queen was apparently delighted when Lord Palmerston (whose nick name was Pammie) was Prime Minister no more. She tried to have someone else as her PM – I always thought these people were selected in Parliament but there I am pretty ignorant about such matters as I am only a lowly servant but she had to have him cos he was so popular. Then he wasnt no more so they chucked

him out . She was pleased because he tried to seduce one of her Majesty's ladys in waiting and that did not please her at all! I hope that you dont show my letters to anyone else. I do run on in them don't I?"

I said that 1866 was a year that meant a great deal to me. I must just add before I leave it that it was also the year when I met a Mr Collins who seemed very interested in my tales of India. I'm afraid that I have a confession to make here for one evening, as I had taken rather too much claret, my tongue ran away with me and I played the 'Old India Hand' with my dark tales of that country. Not that they were untrue you understand, just embroidered a small amount in order to make them that little bit more interesting. I tell you this as I was to read "The Moonstone" a few years later where some of my notions about rascally Indians who came to England to seek a gold statue that has been stolen from a temple have been adapted. Of course I was never at Seringapatam in 1799 with General Baird when the British army looted so much. That was another piece of my embroidery. I must say here however that I do admire the way that Collins used historical fact to such effect in his narrative.

PART THREE

Preparation and Conclusion

Chapter 18

1867-1878

Before his appointed time, a person cannot die though thrown into the very jaws of death; but when that time arrives, even a straw destroys him.

With my leave over I returned to India where I knew that my task was now to find a reliable person that we could in due course arrange to have introduced into the Queen's household. Time was on my side because I had been told that my task was one that need not be rushed, so I was able to wait until 1874 when I discussed this with several persons including Major Edward Bradford, who had been made the General Superintendent of the Thuggee and Dacoit Department. By now it was no surprise to me that this department had been turned into the Viceroy of India's secret police.

But I was surprised to have been asked to come to Bradford's office to see him by himself. I had thought that he might have left this task to an underling. It was the first time that I had actually met him, but I knew him by repute, of course. He was charming to me and said, after he asked me to sit down:

"Well you see even an old crock like me has his uses."

I knew about his lost left arm, and I also knew that he had had to take a spell of leave in England before that as he had worn himself out in the army's service, so I murmured something anodyne. He went on:

"Water under the bridge, dear chap. Now down to business. This is a damned ticklish business and that's why we've chosen you. You have a reputation for keeping your mouth shut. Even after that unfortunate episode with your housekeeper you never said a word."

I must have looked startled for he gave a throaty laugh.

"Now, I shall be I touch with you from now on either to hear how everything is going on or to give you instructions. I must warn you that in order for you to carry this through we will probably pass you over for promotion so as to keep you in obscurity. Sorry about that. Can't be helped. Fortunes of war, and all that. Just think of it this way, we could have lost you in '57 in the uprising. You survived, thanks to that chap Hollowell."

Again that throaty laugh.

"By the way, we knew what you were up to at Lucknow. Too bad that they wouldn't listen to you eh? It just was not on he cards for us to show our hand so we were very grateful to Hollowell. Incidently you may not know it but we've got him into the Corps of Commissionaires. Jolly useful what he hears and passes on to us."

Well that was my future settled. I was to remain in use but out of sight. We then went on to talk about a suitable candidate, and as the Colonel agreed with my choice I was about to make a note to that effect when he stopped me.

167

"No, no notes. Just remember what I said. I certainly shall."

This time the throaty laugh that arrived after he spoke held a note of menace. I thought that this was odd, but who was I to query the old boy's decision?

I was supposed to be in use but not too conspicuous so I tried to be an ordinary soldier and occasionally did extraordinary things. Mind you, I nearly got caught in that business when we had trouble in Abyssinia in 1868. After a deal of shilly-shallying the government, by which I mean Disraeli of course, decided that something had to be done about those poor souls who had been taken hostage. In the hope of dealing with the estimated costs of a rescue which were astronomical, they (Disraeli) decided that the troops in India could be sent to Abyssinia. In that way it would look as if the British Government were not really having to shell out.

So I was sent down to Bombay to assist with the organisation and despatch of men, mules, horses and elephants. Elephants? Yes, it was deemed too difficult to carry our guns through Africa into Abyssinia by any other means than using these huge beasts. The gibes that came my way as I worked in Bombay, for somehow or other it always fell to me to deal with the elephants. For a while I was known as Hannibal Driscoll as I toiled to gather the pachyderms and their mahouts together and then organise their safe loading, not to mention making arrangements for the immense amount of food they consumed, the elephants, not the mahouts. As to dealing with the equally large amount of elephant dung! I'll say no more.

I had seen horses swung onto and off ships in the Russian war and knew how dangerous that could be so I was especially careful, but my best efforts were directed not at seeing that everything went smoothly, but at trying to ensure that I was not included in the troops that went with the damned elephants to Zula on the Red Sea. Please try to understand my situation. I had a job to do and anything that got in the way of that had to be avoided if at all possible. At the same time I was supposed to appear to be employed on the normal activities of some in the army.

One hot evening after a particularly troublesome day when a bolting horse had caused untold mischief, I sat on the verandah with my chotah peg and poured out my troubles to an aide who said that the person to whom I should really be speaking was Forbes-Bosely. He was in charge of all the dispositions. Now I thought I had the answer to the sudden strange decision that had been taken to send me to Bombay. Forbes-Bosely had seized the opportunity to get me attached to an undertaking that many, if indeed, not all considered doomed to failure.

That night I sat and thought about what to do. The following night in the mess I made a point of saying how pleased I was to be attached to an enterprise that offered the opportunity of gaining honour and glory, and that I was looking forward to assisting Britain to strike an honourable blow in support of the poor wretches etc etc. Several comrades looked at me as if I had got a touch of the sun and I knew that my words would be repeated. Once Forbes-Bosely heard them I also knew that he would do his damnest to stop me going, so I went to bed that night mighty pleased with my little stratagem.

Two days later as I stood in the docks surrounded by bedlam and elephant dung I was handed a chitty. I thrust it into my pocket too engaged in my Hannibal tasks to read it.

169

Later on when I had more time I took it out, smoothed out its scrunched up surface and read to my horror that it was confirmed that I was to be attached to the main party that was to depart for Alexandria within two days. Quite unknown to me Forbes-Bosely had fallen sick and his replacement had taken my brave words at face value.

Messages from me to those who I knew could release me from this error went unheeded, so it was in the blackest of moods that I joined a steam ship in the harbour along with a dozen elephants on the 21st of December 1867.

My deliverance came when an elephant went musth, in other words 'mad'. This happens occasionally and whole villages have been known to be destroyed by a bull elephant in this state. Some think that it's a reaction to being in captivity, but whatever the reason it's highly dangerous. Because I was nominally in charge of this outbreak, which I have to admit was successfully dealt with by the elephant's mahout, the authorities were able to use this as an excuse to keep me in India. I was therefore able to quit Bombay and continue with my preparation over the next nine years or so of Abdul Karim for his later activities.

To most people's surprise, except those that had an almost religious belief in Sir Robert Napier who had been appointed Commander in Chief, the whole expedition was a wild success. It so happened that I had to be in Portsmouth in June when the victorious British troops came back; the Indian contingents had been sent back to India. There I got caught up in the enthusiastic noisy raucous crowds that were pushing down to the harbour's edge. I was nearly toppled over by them and was only saved by a dock worker whose rough hand caught my coat saving me from a nasty fall into the muddy gutter. I lost a button as a result but counted that a price worth paying.

He bellowed drunkenly in my ear as he threw his meaty arm around me causing me to shrink away somewhat from his armpit:

"We showed 'em din we?"

His female companion, his wife I supposed, who had drunk as much as her husband judging by her red face and extremely unsteady gait, screamed:

"The brish lines not dead. Not by a long chalk."

The young woman with them tried to pull them away from me. She smiled apologetically and said something that I did not catch. I wanted to ask them what they thought about the Indian troops so I arranged with to meet them later on in a tavern where I had taken a room. I kept my appointment but only the young woman joined me. She was their daughter and she explained that the ale and excitement had been too much for her mother so her parents had gone home. She was nervous and I could quite see why for the drunken crowd were enough to make even me wary. I accordingly suggested that we took ourselves to my room where we could at least hear one another speak.

She assented and we were soon at ease as a servant girl brought me the meal that I had previously ordered. We shared it and I was amused at the vast amount that Dorothy, for such was her name, ate.

"You look at me in surprise. Your surprise would not exist if you knew how infrequently I can eat such a meal. In fact I must own that it is not unusual for me to go for days with little or nothing to put inside me."

In embarrassment I lifted my glass and drank deeply.

"Tell me", I said, what do you and your parents think about this victory?"

She put her head on one side and replied:

"Oh they think that it is splendid. After that terrible business in Afghanistan, and then that dreadful muddle in Balaclava and all, not to speak of the mutiny. Why everyone, even the queen herself says that at last we are in charge of the Empire as we should be."

I was astounded. I had not imagined that I should get such an answer. She looked at me and said:

"You must not think that just because we are poor we do not know what is happening in the world. I can read. I read the London Illustrated News because my missus and master take it and they pass it onto me. They are kind to me in their fashion, even though I am only a skivvy."

She went on somewhat bitterly:

"Unfortunately, while I am never out of a place as a skivvy, my pa only works when there is work to be had in the docks, so the broken meats that I get from my mistress I takes home where I pretend that I have already eaten."

I opened the door and the roar of the crowd below was such that I only managed with some difficulty to call for some more wine. It was brought by a harassed maid. I poured some for Dorothy and myself and sat back to listen to her, for her grasp of what was going on in the world amazed me. Once or twice I ventured an opinion that she challenged vehemently quoting from The Illustrated London News or 'The Thunderer'. Her heroes were Russell and Stanley, those bold reporters who had told the world about our shortcomings in the Crimea and victories in Abyssnia. I'm afraid that she took my interest in her utterances as an indication that I saw her as my intellectual equal, a situation that I was loth to deny as I so enjoyed her company.

I said so. Her eyes brightened. It was not with pleasure at my thoughtfulness though, but the beginnings of tears. For all her bravado she was, after all, only a woman.

I crossed the room and put my arm around her as I too felt tears prick against my eyelids. I honestly only meant to comfort her but she turned to me, clutching me and saying:

"Sometimes the likes of you are kinder to your dogs than you are to likes of us, your poor servants. I will tell you something now that might shock you. My master and mistress being away I stole into their rooms with some hot water and not only did I wash myself all over with it but I used their perfumed soap as well."

It was this confession and the fact that she did indeed smell so much sweeter than many of her ilk that made me return her embrace. You must believe that, for what happened next was not what I had in mind. With downcast gaze and flushed cheeks she said:

"You have paid me the great compliment of treating me as an equal and I would return that compliment with the only gift that a poor girl such as I am has to bestow upon a gentleman such as you are. I pray that you do not spurn my gift."

She stood and removed her garments leaving me in no doubt as to the content of her gift. I was torn between behaving as a gentleman by asking her to leave, and accepting her generous offer. Which action should I take? What did I do, you ask? I can only say that the quality of her gift matched the quality of her generous spirit, and when I woke the following day she was gone.

1878 saw me again in Kabul, this time in disguise, where I saw both Abdul Karim and Haji Wuzeeruddin. I was pleased to note that Haji Wuzeeruddin had accepted my suggestion that Abdul Karim be given a broad experience and was travelling widely with him. He needed a good education if we were to get him into place.

I had to return quickly from Kabul as I received a message that my wife Caroline was unwell. Despite my haste I was too late to comfort her as she passed from this world into the next. In a country where a man can be eating tiffin with you and dead that very evening and buried the next day, we all had to get used to death being our constant companion. Indeed as a soldier, albeit one who hardly ever drew a sword except in salute, early death marched alongside me throughout my career. So it was with my Caroline: one day she was there brightening everyone's life and the next she was gone adding to the numerous deaths that saddened us all. Perhaps it was all for the best, for increasingly her behaviour, 'tho entrancing, had a certain hectic aspect to it that worried me. Indeed the doctor whom I asked about her behaviour hinted obscurely to me as to female proclivities with matters associated with hysteria.

I said here that my wife went from this world into the next but I have to say that my belief at this time in another better world was shaken as was my belief in a benevolent deity. My thoughts were somewhat crystallised by being reminded by a Buddhist monk who had come begging with his chela, that this world was no more than an illusion. I gave him some trifling coins so he expounded on his beliefs. This made me recall Dr Johnson's riposte to the idea of the non-existence of matter that Bishop Berkeley's ingenious sophistry had sought to prove. Boswell, that clever man who had such a reputation as a lecher, wrote that he observed to Dr Johnson, that though we are satisfied that Bishop Berkeley's doctrine is not true, it is impossible to refute it. He then went on to say that he would never forget the alacrity with which Dr Johnson answered him; Johnson struck his foot with mighty force against a large stone, till he rebounded from it, saying as he did so: 'I refute it thus'.

So it was with me. I knew that were I to go to Australia, that sad experiment of dealing with British malcontents, I would find there exactly what others would find. Whereas no one knows where we go once we leave this world. This does not stop many from asserting that they do know. They don't. They only believe they know. In other words, the possible world to come is the illusion, or rather one of several illusions, according to who is talking to you.

I choose for my example Australia because, although I have alluded to James Boswell's reputation as a lecher, mainly as a result of his honesty in his diaries, he was strangely kind to

Mary Bryant, the Cornish lass who escaped from the penal colony in Australia. He represented her at her trial when, having escaped but being recaptured, she was on trial for returning to England. Afterwards he got her a pension so that she could live out her days in Cornwall. I was indebted to Joan Biddlesworth for all these, and other facts. Joan not only made sure that a steady supply of books came from England to her, but passed them onto me. Thus I read selectively, for I only read what she supplied, but also widely, for her interests ranged across many literature frontiers. There were times as a result when I thought that she was almost clever enough to be a man.

Despite my reading I had plenty of time to continue to monitor Abdul Karim and send reports on his progress to Major Bradford. I was not as surprised as some when in 1878 the Major was appointed Governor-General's Agent for Rajputana and Chief Commissioner of Ajmer. It was a subtle move for it meant that he was now overseeing all the relationships between the India Office and all the Raiput princes. I sent him congatulations when he was promoted to Lieutenant Colonel and an aide with fluffy mutton chop whiskers came to see me to acknowledge my card. The aide came instead of Bradford as his master was too caught up in some damn fool business, I was told. The aide and I had drinks during which he confided to me that the 'old man' disliked the princes intensely. The newly appointed Lieutenant Colonel was very amused when I conveyed back to him what his aide had told me about the Raiput princes, namely:

"He thinks they are a lazy lot, good for nothng, vain as peacocks with about as much brain as one. He says he would not trust them to polish his spurs. They are continually plotting and don't know the 'old man' makes sure that he hears everything ."

In 1880 I was sent to join the march to Kandahar. This was that famous forced march that gave General Roberts such a tremendous victory. I was not sent to participate in that march as such; you may know that it was the one that ended the second war against Afghanistan. As I said, I was not there to take part, but instead to keep an eye on Abdul Karim who was also there along with Haji Wuzeeruddin; Haji Wuzeeruddin had been sent there as a medical aide. We still had to be wary of those damn Russians too, but this time they kept out of it.

The march was an exercise in dogged determination. Because of the intense heat we rose early each day to resume our march and by midday stopped, by which time many had fallen out and reported sick. Used as I was to the heat of India I managed better than most, but even I found it a trial. In this fashion and supported by camels that brought up supplies we usually covered about twenty miles a day. Can you imagine it? Moving that huge cavalcade through the extreme heat of day and bitter cold of night, for with no cloud cover the temperature dropped each night like lead from a shot tower. My admiration went less to the participants in the march, although they certainly deserved it, and more to the commissariat that kept us supplied. Without them we should have come to shuddering halt. Most of the real work was done by NCOs but of course officers were nominally in charge. I met one of them.

During that march I was to share a tent several times with a Lieutenant Hector MacDonald who seemed to avoid most of the other officers. I asked around and found that he was a martial phenomenon. Having risen through the ranks he had been offered a commission because of his bravery (some said foolhardy behaviour - but is there any difference?), then he had shown a complete lack of judgement because he accepted it!

177

Now, like a terrier that is included in a pack of hounds he was always ill at ease. He knew that he could do what the other dogs did, possibly better, but also knew that he did not belong there with them. They were thoroughbreds, and to them he was a mongrel. His accent betrayed him despite his attempts to adopt the clipped utterances of his fellow officers. They admired his bravery and despised his background.

I thought that it was the greatest of pities that he had accepted the commission. He would have been a splendid Regimental Sergeant Major lording it in the Sergeants' Mess. I also thought that in due course in order to prove himself he would probably do even wilder braver actions and so get himself killed. I was to be proved wrong. He took to me, largely because I too had not come from a privileged background, but even so I always found him strange. On one occasion I had to wake him up for he was obviously in the grip of a nightmare. He started up at me with an oath, probably Gaelic, and for a moment we grappled together for I think he was still half asleep and was dreaming that I was an enemy. Then he woke up completely and shook me off. He looked ghastly. I had heard him muttering a name in his sleep so to calm him I asked him who Christina was. Once again he started up but this time it was to put his hand over my mouth.

"Shut your gob will ye. Where the de'il did you hear that name?"

"From you. You called it out in your sleep."

He slumped back.

"Look here old chap", I said...

178

"Nae you look here", he began, then groaned and said:

"Oh God whit's the use?"

One thing that I learned fairly quickly in my career was the power of silence. I also knew how to wait.

Eventually after some time without looking at me he began to speak.

"I want to tell you something. I cannae tell the others. No one must know, but I think I shall burst if I don't tell someone. I'm married and I might have a bairn. My wife is Christina. I expect that you know that I am only supposed to get married with permission, and I didnae get it. If I had asked they would have said yes, no doot, but then where would that have got me? I'll tell ye, on permanent garrison duties, that's whuir."

I sympathised with him. There was no promotion to be got in garrisons.

"I cannae tell you the whys and wherefores of it all. And I'm not telling you so you can give me advice d'ye ken?"

I said nothing and eventually it all came tumbling out; the usual story of a man and a maid. This time though it had the extra dimension of a strange undercurrent of something more passionate than just that which he had described as happening between him and his Christina. Only very much later when he had become Major-General Sir Hector Macdonald DSO KCB, did I finally learn about the feet of clay that this idol (they came to call him Fighting Mac) possessed.

Nevertheless I wished him well when we parted at Kandahar, for up to then he had not managed to get himself killed. I watched his progress over the years and even met him again, which particular meeting nearly proved my undoing. But, more of that later.

When I reported back to Lieutenant-Colonel Edward Bradford, my one-time chief at the Thuggee and Dacoit Department, he gave me quite specific instructions about Abdul. As I expected, these were verbal instructions and I was enjoined not to write anything down. As I have already said, Edward Bradford was now the Governor-General's Agent for Rajputana and Chief Commissioner of Ajmer. This post was a front of course to cover all his other activities. My instructions were for me to get Karim employed by the Nawab of Jawara as a Naib Wakil. This I did with no trouble. Obviously my way to achieve this had been smoothed, no doubt with a liberal amount of rupees. After Abdul Karim had worked there for a while I went to see him.

"You have done very well", I told him.

He looked puzzled for we had never met formally and I was a complete stranger to him for I had made sure up to now that this was the case. Nevertheless he was polite and accepted the compliment. At last it was time to tell him more about the plans that had been made for his future. I did so, much to his astonishment. He was less ready however to accept my suggestion that he should now resign his post and join his family in a job as a clerk in the Agra jail-khana as he saw this as a step down. Once I had revealed certain facts to him however about his real parentage he accepted the idea and was soon fully employed as a vernacular clerk in Agra jail where he was in daily contact with the jail's superintendent, John Tyler.

John Tyler was the Anglo Indian doctor at the Agra hospital attached to the jail-khana; he was also the superintendent of that establishment, and I knew that once Abdul Karim was employed there it would only be a matter of time before Tyler would respond to my suggestions and I would find somehow to get Abdul Karim into the royal household. All that I had to do now was to wait patiently for news from London that would let me move on.

Chapter 19

1882

Great results can thus be achieved with small forces.

Amelia's letters continued to come regularly. I always responded to them warmly and encouragingly so that she knew that I enjoyed receiving them. In 1882 she wrote the following to me:

'*We had such excitement here because just as her Majesty was leaving the railway station in her carriage to come to the castle she was shot at by a man. Francis Orchard, the Queen's footman who I told you about in one of my previous letters was there and told me all about it not that he needed to for I was able to get into the Town Hall when they started the trial against Roddy Maclean, that's the name of the chap who did the shooting. I couldn't understand most of what was going on, and in any case I had to leave early as I only had a brief amount of time to myself and I wanted to go to the shops for some thread. Francis told me later that the man was sent back to Reading Jail and will come up again later. I will write again when he is sentenced. I expect that he will be sentenced to death by hanging.*

It seems that this Roderick Maclean is a poet who says that he was upset because her Majesty refused to accept one of his poems. I think that he must be mad. The feeling amongst all the servants is that he should be hanged. What if he had hit Ted Dowe the postilion or Jim Hudson the outrider? Or one of those little Eton boys who went for him with their umbrellas? Brave little chaps. It doesn't bear thinking about.

In Amelia's next letter she wrote:

I heard that General Sir Henry Ponsonby whose in charge of us and is a very nice man had to tell her Majesty that the man who shot at her was let off as he was mad. She was terribly upset at first saying that it was an outrage. Then she calmed down and told Sir Henry that it was worth being shot at as so many people have expressed their loyalty to her as a result of the attack. She said it was worth it to see how much she was loved.

I wrote back to say that anything that increased the general public's loyalty to Her Majesty had to be a good thing, but I thought Her Majesty might be stretching this event just a bit too far in citing it as evidence of her popularity. Pleased with my turn of phrase I signed my letter and called in Raj to make sure that it got sent off safely.

Letters continued to come from Amelia. She also wrote about the riot that took place in London in February. Luckily she was not there in London at the time but one of the many men she wrote about in her letters had been. I noticed she often mentioned these men, but there was never a mention of any proposal of marriage. Maybe I am just an old romantic, but it would have been pleasant to hear from her that she was to be wed. She told me in her letter...but perhaps I ought simply to reproduce here what she said in her very own words:

'Albert was full of it. I think secretly he was frightened, but wouldn't ever admit it to a woman of course, not that I would expect him to. He had been in Oxford Street and heard a great noise what afterwards he knew was the sound of all those

men gathered in Trafalgar Square. They were there because they had no jobs and having nothing better to do got drunk and terrorised all the normal people what were there in the Square driving them out. Someone got up and shouted at them that they were poor because the rich made them so. The very idea. There poor cause they won't work, thats the beginning and end of it. They started breaking windows. Of course thats just the way to get the rich to help the poor ain't it? I don't think!!

Albert told me that he was in two minds whether to go then or stay to see what happened next 'curiosity killed the cat' I told him and he said 'satisfaction brought it back! He is a card. He does make me laugh sometimes. Anyway they all come up Oxford Street looking for more windows to break and Albert saw a few take things. That was when things really got ugly, not helped by the police what seemed unable to stop it so got out their staves and began to hit people. When that didn't stop them the police made themselves scarce, not that I blame them. They were only a few and the mob, for it was a mob, just seemed to go mad.

Albert said that he went into a shop where the owner said that he would give him two pounds if he would help put up some shutters. 'The easiest two quid I ever earned.' He then stayed safely behind them listening to the rioting that went on for hours. He was late getting back because of it and got into trouble because of it. He wanted me to be sympathetic, but I weren't having any of that. As my Ma would have said 'He made his bed, so he had to lie on it'. Later on Lizzie told me that he told her all about too and she gave him a hug and he stole a kiss, more fool her I say. I have put in this letter a page from the Pictorial News that shows the riots.'

185

The sheet of pictures that Amelia included were all drawn I imagine by someone who was told what had happened and had used his imagination to depict what he considered the readers would wish to see. I heard in due course that as a result of the police losing control that Sir Charles Warren was called back from abroad to become the Commissioner of the Metropolitan Police. This was the first of a series of changes that resulted eventually in our getting Edward Bradford appointed as the Commissioner! But well before that happened he was knighted as a Knight Commander of the Star of India. Meanwhile, just as he had warned me, I was passed over several times for promotion, much to Forbes-Bosely's delight. I held my tongue and continued to receive letters from Amelia.

But the letter that I really wished to receive from quite another source took much longer to arrive, so I simply let matters follow their natural course. Then on a very wet monsoon day after reading a report that had, at long last, been posted to me, I smiled in great satisfaction and set off to Agra Jail to see the Superintendent. Matters had been most satisfactorily handled in England. It was time for me to make my next move. Shouting to Raj to get me a gharry and find me a chutter that was not too covered in mould for it was raining, I went out onto the veranda to await their arrival.

Joan was with me at the time as she had invited herself to tiffin, and it was curious that she expressed no interest in my report. Of course I realise now that she was such an established figure in the department that she probably already knew what was in it. This was confirmed when the hot season began and she went up to Simla.

Chapter 20

1886

Let no human being be despised, for who can tell how soon even the lowest may be raised

Dr John Tyler was a busy man, but not so busy that he could not find the time to tell me of his experiences in London where he had recently attended the Colonial and Indian Exhibition. He had gone there with a body of carpet weavers from the prison who had woven carpets and were able to demonstrate to the queen herself their skills. As someone who had previously overseen the carriage and exhibition of a similar carpet in 1851, I was interested in his account and I knew that we would get round the point of my visit in due course. I listened patiently as he explained:

"As you know, I am a busy man so I left the choice of carpets that we took to my assistant. He is a most able and intelligent young man. He has not been married long and is a steady example to all who see him. He would have liked to have gone to England too but it was quite out of the question, quite out of the question."

I smiled with satisfaction. My protege had turned out well.

"But John, I understand that before you returned you were asked to find some servants, some Indians who could go to England to assist in the coming Jubilee."

He looked amazed.

" Oh my goodness, how did you know?"

I laughed.

"Oh, come now, you know where I work. Don't try that act with me. You know that I hear all the news and gossip. It's part of my job."

He stroked his chin thoughtfully and looked at me shrewdly.

"So what is your interest in this matter?"

"The same as yours: that is to find some suitable men who will impress the queen and not let down India."

"Well yes. So we have to be very careful."

"Just so. But were you to suggest young Karim as one of the khidmatgars I am sure you would have made an excellent choice."

I waited. Had I acted too quickly? I received another shrewd look.

"Well to tell you truly, I had already thought about him and I had also thought I should send Mohammed Busksh."

He looked at me enquiringly. I nodded. I think we understood one another completely.

"Mohammed Busksh runs your household doesn't he? Can you spare him?"

"If it's for the Queen's Jubilee, of course I can and will.

"John, I hear that it's being said that if these men prove to be suitable that they could be retained which means that you would lose both of them."

He spread his hands expansively and expressively and said:

"As Mohammed Busksh would say 'Inshallah'.

And so it was settled.

Joan sent a message to me from Simla. It was to the effect that it would do me good to get away into the cool of the hills, and there was someone there that she wanted me to see. I noticed that she did not say *meet.* I replied that I was far too busy at the moment.

I had been experimenting with Indian clothing which is much more comfortable than European dress being loose and made of thin cotton. I occasionally ventured out in such a garb, and was delighted to be addressed by most natives in their native tongues, most of which I understood. Of course my replies were not perfect enough to fool them so I pretended that I came from the north of India and had a mother from Nepal. I got myself a puggaree and because I was so often in the sun which coloured my complexion I looked like one of those blue-eyed Pathans. My purpose was not to fool anyone, but rather to melt into the crowd.

Now I dressed up again and thus garbed I travelled up in the poorest class of train compartment along with several ladies in burkas, some coolies and an ancient Moslem gentleman who immediately subjected me to an intense series of questions. At first I tried to pass myself off as coming from the north but he saw through that lie straight away, so I hung my head and whispered that my mother had told me before she died that my father was a firenghi soldier who had gone home. This lie satisfied him. He proceeded to wag his head and finger at me.

"You need not be ashamed of your parents brother. They might have been how you came into this world but Allah, may his name be praised, will decide your fate."

The others in the compartment rumbled agreement with this judgement that was delivered by the ancient solemnly who stroked his whiskers and then smiled benevolently, proud to have penetrated my lies. To his question of why I was travelling I replied that I hoped to get work in Simla and that I had spent the last of my money on my mother's funeral and a ticket. Another rumble of approval met this assertion. I was obviously a good man who met his obligations.

We left the train together, and as we did so, I was shouted at by a policeman who was standing next to a soldier. The policeman said that they wanted to search me.

"Put this into your sandal", said the old man, slipping me some pice. I knelt before the policeman and in pretence of salaaming him I did as the old man had told me. The soldier had not seen me get the cash but noticed that I had touched my sandal and said:

"Right you black bastard thief, you misbegotten son of a rancid whore, what have you got there?"

I stayed silent so he pushed me down and pulled off my sandal letting the pice fall out.

"Well, so you are a thief", he said gathering them up.

He kicked me, pocketed the money after giving some of it to the policeman, and told me to bugger off samjao? I was about to say something when the old man caught my eye and shook his head saying quietly:

"Gently brother, gently."

I walked on thinking that at least the incident showed me that my disguise was a good one. Luckily he had not thought to root around in my puggaree where I had spent the previous evening sewing in some rupees, but I think my breath perfumed with the native food that had been pressed upon me put him off. The white civilians who were walking by ignored me. Those that came close to me held their handkerchiefs to their noses averting their eyes so proving to me that I not only looked like a coolie but smelled like one too.

From a small hill town Simla has expanded immensely with its bazaar spreading like a growth on the side of the hill providing housing, shops, eating places for all castes and God alone knows what else for all sorts of inhabitants. I plunged into it savouring the noise, smell and constant exchange of insults that seems to be an essential part of life in India.

The eternal verbal give and take of insulting one another does not stop when the natives become servants to white people. Many whites have little concept of what their servants were actually saying to them presuming that because the attitude of a dhobi wallah or amah was subservient, their comments in the vernacular were also subservient. It amused me immensely on occasions to see white memsahibs, who were newly come out from England and had mastered enough native words to give orders, smile beatifically as their servants insulted them, smiling as they did so.

I found a convenient wall against which to lean in the shade until Ahmed joined me. He had been warned that I was coming and already knew the man that Joan had wanted me to *see.* From the description that Ahmed gave me of him I immediately suspected that he was a spy so I told Ahmed that he and two others were to get him to come to a room in the bazaar where I would wait to see him for myself.

As I waited I kept in the shadows of a dirty back room with a beaten mud floor that was down in the least salubrious part of the bazaar. I was amongst the huqa smokers but did not try one. He came in and was seated on a charpoy against the wall where I could study him for there were no seats of course. He looked around seemingly completely at his ease. He looked like a horse dealer, and smelled as such.

I listened as Ahmed talked to him. Eventually I decided that I would try to shock him so I came from the shadows and unwound the cloth from my face and said in English:

"Come now, tell us who you really are?"

His head came up. He smiled and replied in perfect English:

"My dear chap. I can no more reveal that to you than you can tell me just who you really are in this company! But, I know you, yes I know you."

"My God! You're..." I began.

His lifted hand stopped me just as I was about to say his name out loud. Under my breath I muttered 'Strickland – Inspector Strickland'.

One of my men said in Urdu:

"What did you say O highest one?"

I replied in Urdu:

"Nothing. I said nothing. Please leave us now."

They looked at one another, obviously puzzled so I said Rather more loudly than I intended:

"You have done well. Now I must talk alone with this man."

I told the owners of the premises to bring us some food which they did and we sat crossed-legged upon the floor native fashion eating together the rice and vegetables completely at ease now that we had both established each others identity. I knew Inspector Strickland of old of course. His exploits when he became various characters, and in such disguises caught badmashes by such subterfuges were well known. He was feared as a result, or had been for I thought that he had ben forbidden to do this any more.

"But inspector, I thought that your days of infiltrating the bazaars like this were over?"

" Yes, you're quite right. I gave it up. This particular outing is to help some chap to whom I owe a good turn. It's not a criminal matter."

He paused and smiled. I waited.

"Surely you don't expect me to say any more?" he asked.

"After all, the whole essence your work is to say as little as possible, so you must as a result think that my reticence is to be applauded."

I bowed my head in agreement. My satisfaction at finding that my suspect was Strickland and not a Russian spy meant that naturally I was willing not to pursue the matter. Besides, now that I had a name I expected that Joan would get all the details. And I was right. No, I cannot say more even at this distance in time. Suffice to say that by his activity Strickland repaid his debt and put right a wrong that could not otherwise be righted and so prevented a terrible festering of spirit.

I said goodbye and made my way back to await news of the two kitmanders who were to be introduced into the service of the queen.

Chapter 21

1887

Trust a Brahmin before a snake, and a snake before an harlot and an harlot before a Pathan

I heard that from the very beginning that both men made a deep impression. Amelia wrote one of her usual letters and in it she said:

'As if the Jubilee celebrations ain't caused enough trouble and excitement for us we now have two Hindoos wished on us. Not everyone is pleased that they have been sent to be servants. There is talk that perhaps English servants should be given more responsibility. But they do look swell in their uniforms and Josephine what works with me says that they look like princes. She has read a book called The Arabian Nights Entertainments and says that these two men could have stepped out of one of the stories. One is stout and jolly and the other one is more serious.'

Abdul certainly lost no time in getting his own way. Having impressed the queen he proceeded to do some cooking. Amelia wrote in her letter:

'It was Minnie who told me the whole story. The hindoos, bold as brass, simply marched into the kitchen and said that they were going to cook some native dishes. Chef was really upset but General Dennehy told him that they were to be left alone. The General speaks their lingo and is in charge of the hindoos. The smells were really pungent I can tell you. I expect that you are used to such smells, but it was a real shock to everyone here to smell their spices and kurry.'

Later on she wrote again:

'Christmas at Osborne House is always very special and I go to bed at the end of Christmas day thinking of my dear Ma and Pa what would have been so pleased to see me in such company at this time of year never mind that I am in service, for look who I am in service to as Minnie says. To be honest I do weep a little before I goes to sleep specially if I have a little wine what we servants get as its Christmas. The hindoos don't get no wine for their religion says they must not drink.

Those black hindoos seemed to be amazed at the tree and all so we asked them did they not have Christmas in India to which the fat one said that they did and it was called bada din. The tall good looking one despite he is a heathen did not say a word. I know he can speak English but he is so proud.'

In her next letter she wrote:

'Oh the upsets that we are going through because of that man, not the fat one, he's nice and pleasant to everyone and knows his place. It's the tall proud one. It's not that I have anything to do with him. I'm too lowly for the likes of him, but when he upsets the others, even Sir Henry I hear is put out, everyone gets at sixes and sevens. He's not at all like those two hindoos that you brought with you to Surbiton that time when my Ma died. They were really nice. I expect it was because you had trained them up so well. They did upset Cook though, I remember Mama telling me about them the first day that she was employed by you.'

I became uneasy. Had I told Abdul too much about his parentage? Perhaps it might have been better not to have revealed to him his connection with me. I had sworn him to secrecy about this but I began to think that knowing what he did had made him conceited. Luckily no one else knew about my connection with Abdul although I realised that I might have to confess to it in time. Actually someone else did know: Haji Wuzeeruddin, but I was sure that the money that I had given him had been sufficient to ensure that he maintained a discreet silence. The only other person who might have suspected the truth was my wife. I felt a twinge of guilt as I thought of her; not at having been too late to comfort her as she passed from this vale of tears to a better life, but at the thought that luckily with her death no one now knew about my secret.

I knew that Bradford had returned to London as Secretary of the Political and Secret Department of the India Office. This strengthened my belief that the work that I was engaged in was still likely to be supported from that quarter although I had not recently heard anything to that effect.

What I did hear though was that Younghusband had gone off on leave with another young chap, Henry James, who was in the Indian Civil Service along with Harry Fulford who was a British consular officer to 'explore' parts of Manchuria. Now young Younghusband is a damned clever cove whose skills at mapmaking and other scientific abilities are able to cover his real work which is to do work that we can't do officially. We know that the Russians are also doing this and, I don't doubt, using Russian gold to make friends with the natives. A very shrewd move not to let Younghusband go off by himself. If he went on his own we would only have his account of what he got up to. You see. Once you get into this game, it's best not to trust anyone unless you are absolutely sure of them.

Chapter 22

1888-1889

Every one looking downwards becomes impressed with ideas of his own greatness; but looking upwards, feels his own littleness.

Amelia's latest letter to me told me what I already knew, that Ahmed Hussain had arrived. She also told me that Abdul had come back to India for a holiday.

'Would you believe it? Another one of those Indian Hindoos has come to work here. Tim says what's wrong with employing Englishmen? They don't eat any of what we have, preferring their own stuff what they cook themselves. This ones called Hussain. He is friendly enough.' Not like that Abdul what treats us all with disdain while sucking up to all the gentry. He seems to think that if he goes on this way that he will be like them, some hopes!

'It's not right. Every time we look at the newspapers there seems to be as much about the Indians and their turbans and all that as about the rest of the household. And that Abdul has a special title now and has been put in charge of the Indians not that they like that. We have been told to forget that he came to wait on table and I heard tell that any picture of him doing that have been burned.

The tall Indian who has somehow wormed his way into Her Majesty's good books has gone back to India. We all said good riddance only to hear that he was going home for a holiday and would be coming back. I'm afraid that the whole household is upset and unsettled because of this chap that we have to call Munshi. I think it's a funny name to call anyone, more like a name you might give to a pet dog. That's what I said to Minnie who said that Munshi means teacher, so why don't we call him teacher then I asked but she had no answer to that. He does give himself such airs and graces you would think he was more important than a common servant. Francis made me laugh when he said...

This next part was scribbled out

I don't think that what Francis called him was fit for a ladys' ears. I know I ain't one, but still I've scratched it out.

The police have still not caught that murderer who calls himself Jack the Ripper. I expect you know all about it on account of you being in with Scotland Yard and all. I remember that time when we were all in Surbiton and my Ma and you was seeing that Jack Witcher who was so clever you said. I expect tho that he has retired to a country cottage now but if they was to call him back he would find out who he is, the Ripper I mean. I'm glad that I don't go out that often in London with him walking the streets. Not that I would go out at night by myself. I can't think what any right minded young woman would. I can't tell you what Francis said when I said that. Leastways I'd better not. Nor should I repeat gossip about Prince Albert Victor who you might see cos he is coming to India on a tour, but it's so stupid that it can't be true anyway so I can tell you. Francis says that the reason they ain't caught the ripper is cos he is someone important, so important that they are hiding who it is until he can be got away to stop him. And who, says Francis is being taken to India who is important???

It was disturbing, to say the very least, to hear that Bradford had returned to India to conduct Prince Albert Victor, Duke of Clarence on a tour of the country. What was going on? I soon heard. I was called to a meeting where it was decided who was to meet Prince Albert Victor when he reached Bombay. To my utter amazement I was chosen! I duly presented myself to the palace of the Nizam of Hyderabad who was to be the first to play host to the prince. There I was immediately whisked by gharry to a seedy office in a nearby street.

"Very pleased to meet you again", said a familiar croaky voice and Bradford came into the room where I had been led. He looked much older, drawn and fatigued.

"Sit down , sit down", he said, doing so himself looking at me thoughtfully as he did so.

"You ain't such a dolt as you expected to be brought here to meet the prince? Thought not. Well, let's get down to brass tacks. First off, forget all this nonsense about the Ripper. Next, forget what you might have heard about Cleveland Street. We have managed to clear up that mess; someone, you don't need to know who, has had to pay the price, but he will be reinstated in time. All you need to know is that we thought it was advisable that our dear prince should be out of the British public's eye for a while."

So it was true, those rumours. I had dismissed them when I had heard about that place and Lord Arthur Somerset. I had assumed that it was only Lord Arthur who was involved, and that his solicitor had cooked up some false evidence to implicate the prince. Now that the prince had been whirled away to our shores I was not so sure that the evidence had been falsified. I kept silent. Better to say nothing and have people take you for a fool rather than open your mouth and remove all doubt.

"But that's not why I wanted to see you. It's this Abdul. It's time we let some others into what we have been planning. I have called together some chaps here in India to listen to you say what you have accomplished so far. You don't need to know why it's politic to take this line of action just now; all you have to do is tell them. No need to say how I fit into the picture, by the way" he added nonchalantly as he stood up rather shakily and left.

So that was it. I was to implicate myself. I suppose that if we were successful then everything would be fine. If, on the other hand, it failed, it was clear who would have to take the blame.

Of course I did exactly as he said. I had no choice in the matter. Actually, it was useful to have others in the know; if everything did come crashing down I might have others to share the blame with me. The cunning old bastard. No notes, he had said, so nothing led back to him. I resolved however to follow Prince Albert Victor's progress for I wondered whether it was really necessary for him to be accompanied by Bradford as he did his tour. Were they protecting him? Or were they scared that he might go off the rails in India?

He was entertained wherever he went, usually travelling by train in compartments that had been done up special to suit a prince, but occasionally, to the delight of the natives who love a show, he moved along on an elephant that was all dressed up in the usual garish way with little mirrors sewn into cloth coverings. I saw pictures of him smiling and waving as his mahout prodded the great beast with his anka. He even bagged a tiger that had been driven towards him on his elephant so that he could take a potshot at it.

I actually saw him on one occasion. It was a terribly hot afternoon and he did not look at all comfortable, and when the elephant was made to kneel so that he could step out of the howdah he looked as if he couldn't wait to leave it. I heard later that he had been told how men who had been sentenced to death were sometimes trodden on by an elephant to execute them. It might have unsettled him. Brown hands were thrust towards him as he scrambled out and almost ran to he door of the hotel where he was staying. A striking looking white woman dressed all in white with an embroidered parasol in one had held out the other slim pale hand to him and he took it.

I asked who she was and I was told that she was Mrs. Margery Haddon, the wife of a civil engineer. I made a few more enquiries and found that our prince had found a friend. I wondered whether this was an elaborate ruse to establish him as a man who liked women. Apparently he liked Margery Haddon enough set in train another scandal.

Chapter 23

1889

There's no Fool Like an Old Fool.

I'm afraid that Abdul was still not trying hard enough to influence others in the royal household other than the queen. I knew that he thought that as he had her ear he really did not need to bother with any others, but if he continued to go on in this way I was afraid that he might go too far and ruin our plans. Amelia wrote to tell me about moving up the limited ladder of promotion that was available to her as a woman servant. She also told me how Abdul was acting like a veritable prima donna. Oh dear!

We had a special treat when a theatrical company came up to Sandringham (yes I move about now when the household moves-someone seems to have noticed my good work, as my Ma frequently said to me know you place and always do your best and you will not regret it, nor do I) This company came to put on a show called THE BELLS. The treat for us was we were all allowed to sit at the back behind everyone that mattered and watch the show. I liked it but was a bit frightened too but Edward held my hand until Minnie saw him then he let go smartish. All the same I did enjoy it. The Bells I mean well I suppose that I enjoyed Edward's attention as well. Despite his station in life life he knows how to behave like a true gent that's why Minnie likes him she says.

It was nearly spoiled tho for the tall hindoo made a fuss when he found that he was supposed to sit with us. Ahmed Hussain was there and sat quietly along with all of us servants as he was meant to but Mr high and mighty stalked off in a huff. I heard that he went to his room and would not come out although the nice fat hindoo entreated him. I think he makes a fuss so that everybody has to pay attention to him. I bet he would not get away with it if her majesty got tired of him. She seems to be fassinated with him and everything Indian. I imagine that you understand this, working with them as you do but for the life of me I fail to understand how he does it. He's getting fat too and I think that he is losing his looks. Maybe I should not have written that as it aint Christian is it to say such things of people but speak as you find says Millie.

Just because he teaches her Majesty his heathen lingo doesn't mean that he's any better than us. And he's not a Christian neither. When he refused the other day to sit with the servants where his real place is, and instead stalked off like a little boy and sulked I thought right my lad if my Pa was alive and saw such behaviour he'd say he ought have his backside tanned. The trouble is her Majesty dotes on him! He can do no wrong. He's quite turned her head. I know that I should not say it but I will any way There's no Fool like an Old Fool. I remember that I heard my ma said that to you once. I wonder if you remember that?

I did indeed remember that episode. How often I had tried without success to expunge it from my memory, not because I took offence when I heard it, but because it brought back memories of someone who is now lost to me.

I replied to Amelia and I must have been more encouraging than usual for she wrote again to me almost immediately. Maybe it was just the sensational news that she had to impart.

I can't hardly believe what I have got to tell you about in this letter. That Moonchi has a brother in law and he has been stealing from the Queen. He's a thief. It was Eileen what told me the story. Her Majesty was being taken out and needed a brooch to fasten a shawl about her. Somehow the brooch weren't fastened properly and it fell down on the ground. He was caught because he found it and silly man sold it to a pawnbroker in Windsor. I know the shop as I have looked in his window that time when I thought someone might want to buy me something but that's all over now. I ain't going to say any more about that, that's for sure. Any way the Moonchis brother in law Hourmet Ali is his name didn't know that the pawnbroker was suspicious of him, and quite rightly too how does someone like him get a brooch like that?

The pawnbroker comes to the office in the castle where they deal with supplies where he hands over the brooch and told his story. But would you believe it? That moonchi fellow told the Queen that in his country if you found something you kept it. A likely story. Anyway Her Majesty said she believed him. I couldn't believe my ears when I heard that. If I found something and sold it I would be sent packing straight away I can tell you and no mistake.

I said in my last to you that I wasn't going to say no more about that certain person what I wasn't going to mention. WELL I suppose I may as well tell you for to tell the truth I'm feeling really down about this. I really think that I do not have much luck when it comes to men. All the young men what have showed any interest in have been stolen away by prettier women. Bu the final straw was my latest beau. I really thought as how I had finally found someone who never ever looked at another woman and that was the trouble for he was much too friendly with other men if you catch my *meaning, you being a man of the world and all, but I mustn't run on. I just wanted to tell someone for I do feel down I really do.*

Reading Amelia's latest missive left me deflated too, not only because of Abdul's shenanigans, but because of Amelia's depression. I wrote as cheerful letter as I could in which I said that there were many more fish in the sea, but I nearly tore it up when I read it; it seemed so false.

Chapter 24

1890-1893

Who stands still in mud sticks in it

Never mind what I thought was false, it apparently did not appear so to Amelia for she wrote saying how my letter had really cheered her up!

You can't know how Pleased I was that you took my letter so serious. It makes all the difference to me knowing that I can say things to you that I am not able to say to anyone here. I can also tell you all the news here for I know that it interests you to hear all my gossip. Speaking of which I must tell you about Prince Albert Victor, Duke of Clarence, the Prince that was sent to India to keep him out of trouble. Well it seems that despite all in India he found hisself a lady friend who was not enough of a lady to say NO. Now she has come to England saying that she has had a baby and guess who she says is his pa?

They have given the game away by providing her with a clothes allowance. Minnie gave me the details of that. Would they pay her anything if she was a fraud? They are packing her back to India for she was born there. I heard tell tho that she was making it difficult for she says the prince wrote hot letters to her (silly man) and she has them but will take money for them. My feelings are for her baby, but I expect they will arrange things so he (it's a boy) don't want for nothing.

She also gave me other news. It was all about the 'Moonshee', his ill health and his childish behaviour.

With that letter from Amelia telling me about Abdul's health, and expanding on what she had heard about his latest argument that he had when the royal party were abroad in France, I knew that I had to face the others, who now knew about the plan, and make out a case for keeping on with Abdul despite the way he was acting. Amelia's tone was a mixture of glee and righteous indignation.

You see. I knew it. You can't eat that Indian food and stay healthy. Mr High and Mighty has got boils, and perticulary a big one on his neck. The queen's doctor eventually cut it out but not before another doctor was brought in. But that's not all. Her Majesty fusses over him as if he was her son. I'm not alone in thinking that she ought not to be a lowering of herself in this way. It aint right, not at all right.

I must tell you too about the scene that Minnie saw when they were in France. She told me that Ahmed, who has been ill too (too much kurry if you ask me- all those hot spicy foods can't be good for you) was in the corridor and shouted at Mr H and M. They then had a furious row, all in their native lingo of course. Minnie saw Mr H and M go straight off to her Majesty. Meanwhile Ahmed was in tears. They are so like children. They have an argument and the spoiled one runs off to tell Mama.

At the meeting where we discussed my progress so far. I was congratulated again on having a man in place, but inevitably we had one member of the group who raised the problem of the undeniable fact that he is stirring up trouble in the household. My recollection of what was said went as follows:

213

"Does that really matter?" I asked.

"We have a man who seems to have the ear of the queen. Surely that's the important thing."

"We do indeed and surely that counts for more than a few noses being put out of joint", said someone supporting me.

"Well, it rather depends how many he upsets and who they are. Those Ladies in Waiting are no problem. I'm not so sure about Reid or Ponsonby; if they got together and recruited the Prime Minister they could be a considerable force."

"Don't they have any idea of why we have worked so hard to get him into the household?"

"Good God no, it's essential that they know absolutely nothing of our real objectives. Anyway, he's there now. Presumably he was chosen rather than one of the Indian princes on the grounds that no matter which one we chose the others would be jealous and that might have been worse. It's interesting that this chap who started as a waiter then got himself labelled as a munshi seems to be ignored by the princes. I suppose that as they consider he's of no account because he is a simple language teacher he can do what he likes."

There was a pause and, as I supposed it would be, someone, I forget exactly who, raised the matter of Rafiuddin, or to give him his full title and name Ahmed Rafiuddin, Barrister-at-Law. This man had come from India and become a barrister in London. He had got friendly with Karim because Karim had the ear of Her Majesty. He then worked on Karim to such an extent that Karim persuaded her to give Rafiuddin, not only a picture of herself but also an excerpt from the journal that she and Abdul had written.   I was delighted with this because Rafiuddin, who was also called the Moulvi, had links with the Muslim League. Rafiuddin used the excerpt and photo of the queen to write an article in the Strand magazine. This tickled Her Majesty who after that did what she could to further his career.

This was not the problem however. I was told, what I already knew, namely that others in the Thugee and Dacoity Department were suspicious of Rafiuddin. They thought that he was some sort of spy who sent information through his Indian contacts to Kabul. I tried to allay their fears by saying that Rafiuddin did indeed send information for he was also a journalist, but what he sent was mere gossip, the sort of thing that often appeared in the newspapers. In any case I added, did they really suppose that someone who was favoured by the queen would indulge in such activities that could ruin his whole career were he to be unmasked?

This was the trouble in an organisation like ours that dealt with the collection of information; how to sift out the facts from the rumours. And how to deal with misinformation fed in by malcontents, for I felt that behind this suspicion was the hand of Forbes-Boseley.

In the end it was decided that we should go on much as we had before. I offered a prayer to whichever deity looked after plotters like myself. I rather suspect that Kali would fit the bill. It's a fine balancing act. I have to encourage Abdul to continue his work with the Queen but not to upset the household in the process. Unfortunately although his English is improving, his understanding of the nuances of court relationships leaves a great deal to be desired. To be fair I have to consider how utterly out of place I would be in one of the prince's courts here in India. When I remind myself that somehow he has now got himself into a position where he daily instructs one of the greatest rulers in the western world, and as a result she now writes and speaks a little in a language that is so unlike French, German or English, I marvel. I marvel first at how he has done this, and secondly how steadfast she is in continuing to try to learn at her age. They are both remarkable people in their separate ways. Both with flaws though.

A further letter came from Amelia that surprised me until I read it and realised that she had been given a treat and wanted to share it with me. I always quote from her letters where she mentions Abdul, but I truly believe that were I to put all her letters into a book it would be a most interesting one for, although she is only an unlettered female servant, her observations are extremely sharp and, on occasions, very entertaining. It might be interesting but I fear it would also be impossible to publish; she does 'speak as she finds'!

Because I had finished all my work I was able to go out at the back of the East Lawn to see Buffalow Bill and his troop of rough riders. The whole troop had been brought by train to perform before her Majesty. We heard all the cheering well before they got to the castle because they paraded through the town and everyone in the town turned out to see the free show. Of course the Hindoos were there with the Munchee at the front. There was Indian dances from American Indians who were quite different to the Indians who we have in the Royal Household. I thought that it was going to rain, not that would have stopped the show for her Majesty was in a tent thing, but it held off only staying rather dull which is as usual in Windsor. I could not see that well for I had to stand at the back but I saw most of it and heard it too! There was pretend fighting and what our groom called 'war whoops' He had got hold of a programme so could tell me what was on it. He offered to show it to me if I gave him a kiss. Cheeky devil! The Major General was there and so was Sir Henry. I often see them nowadays because I am trusted so much more having been in her Majesty's employ for twenty-six years now. How time flies!

Yes indeed. Don't it just! It seemed only a few months ago that Captain, Younghusband, as he is now, went off on that expedition to Manchuria. He must have impressed the Department with what he managed to accomplish, for when raiders from Hunza (yes, yes I know you have not the slightest idea where Hunza is, but that's not important) upset everybody who were trying to keep the trade routes open, Younghusband was sent to sort the situation out. Not by himself of course, but with a detachment of Gurkhas. That was the story, and up to a point it was true. What most people did not know though was that Captain Bronislav Grombchevsky, who was Younghusband's mirror image in Russia, was also there so it gave these apparent opponents an opportunity to talk frankly.

We know that it was a frank exchange for there was no note made of what was said. All we know is that both men parted after a convivial evening together, one to go to Tibet, that mysterious country, and Younghusband to Karakorum, the mountain area that borders India and China. And no, we were not concerned that China would be a threat. That empire has had its day. Weakened first by rulers who bled the country dry to serve their pleasures and now in thrall to opium it will never be able to become a major power ever again. But I hope that you just remember what I said about our chaps going out by themselves. Here is Younghusband meeting Bronislav Grombchevsky and we have no record of what it was that they discussed. If I were in charge of things I would be wary of Younghusband and would try to get some idea of that meetng. I would also be very wary of Younghusband if he showed any signs of wanting to go to Tibet.

Chapter 25

1894

Advice to the stupid produces anger

I knew that Abdul had come to India: he had arrived on board the usual mail steamer that came to Bombay. Although by now to the world I was to all intents and purposes retired, I still had most of my old contacts for I had simply been moved to a sub-branch of the Thuggee and Dacoitry Department that didn't technically exist; there were no records kept of that branch that I knew of. I was not even allowed to know its name.

It is not unusual to find that there exists within a secret police and internal secret division; it normally exists to keep an eye on the whole Secret Service in to stop it going out of control. This part that I had been told would give me instructions in future however, seemed to be more concerned with what went on in England. I had my suspicions that the Chief Commissioner of Police in London, Sir Edward Bradford, who had served in India, was kept informed by this particular sub-section.

I could no longer wear uniform now which was a bit sad as, although I do eschew vanity I do also consider that when I was in full fig I really looked a suitable representative of the powers that be, which is as it should be. It felt strange not getting into some form of uniform each day. When I was on furlough in England I naturally dressed in mufti, but resumed my normal regimentals when I returned to India. Now I put aside my colourful garb with some regret in favour of a drab set of clothes. Clad in this apparel and at my age (I do realise that the years have taken their toll on the bright young face that I presented when I first landed in India) I began to disappear! I began to be invisible; I do not mean that literally of course, but where I once had presence and people looked up when I entered a room now no one did. I told myself that this non-identity was just the ticket for me in my new role. That phrase 'just the ticket' was one that I heard when I frequented a music hall in London. I know that it would probably impress you much more if I had told you that I always went to the opera when I was in London. But I didn't. I'm afraid that mostly all that sort of thing bores me to tears. My idea of a good night out was to see Gus Elen at the Hoxton Music Hall singing 'If It Wasn't for the 'Ouses in Between' or Marie Lloyd, whose double entendres brought the house down, with her famous 'Oh! Mr porter what shall I do?' and I would lay a guinea to a farthing that most of the men reading this would agree with me. As to the ladies, God bless them, I shall leave them to the delights of Verdi. Anyway, to return to my new role: I now began to comprehend how servants were ignored, and as a result, overheard so very much.

So I waited, for I not only knew that Abdul had come to India but that he was being shadowed by some of my former colleagues who knew nothing about my interests in him. 'What a cat and mouse game' I thought, or rather: 'lots of cats and only one mouse game'. I bided my time and sure enough Abdul turned up at the spot that I had agreed previously with him. He had given them all the slip. He looked tired.

He told me that 'they' were trying to get rid of him. They were doing it by poisoning the ears of Her Majesty with lies. They had said that he was of no account, a mere waiter who had tricked Her Majesty by pretending to be more than a servant. He asked me whether teaching Her Majesty was not more important than simply waiting upon her. He called upon me and Allah to witness the many honours that she had laid upon him. He asked me to say that he had not been worthy of them all. When I stayed silent he burst out that of course he had earned them. He almost cried with vexation at my silence.

When he at last fell silent I reminded him again of the fact that although he had risen, it had been from very humble beginnings. I too had trodden the same path; I understood his feelings, but we shared a common purpose and we had to put aside our feelings in order to achieve it.

It was about this time that I decided that I should do Joan the great honour of being my wife. I had reached an age where looks in one's wife mattered less than a sturdy pair of arms and legs, for increasingly at the end of the day I felt a great lassitude that was not only occasioned by the wine that I had taken but also I must admit, my age. She would be an ideal woman to care for me as she understood me and all my little ways. She would also love to hear from me all those parts of my life that hitherto I had not yet had time to impart to her. I knew that I would not have to go to the trouble of asking her in any romantic setting for Joan was a sensible woman who would leap at the chance of being married. I also knew that she would come to me with no dowry, but I was ready to accept this sacrifice.

Imagine my astonishment when she declined me! Not only that, but she declined to explain why. I told her in no uncertain terms that rejecting my generous offer meant that she owed me an explanation, a statement that made her laugh! It seems that I have luckily missed being yoked to a woman who has no real understanding of my position and importance in society.   Naturally I did not tell anyone of my proposal and its rejection by Joan; I wished to save her the embarrassment of everyone knowing that she had refused an offer of marriage that would have ensured that she would no longer be pitied, but despised for not jumping at the chance to be married.

Chapter 26

1895

Sex will drag you further than gunpowder can blow you

One great advantage of the queen being to taken up with all things Indian and in perticuler that haughty Indian is that everyone in the household is given the chance to visit the Empire of India Exhibition. Naturally you would know all about everything that's in it that we saw. I went with Eddie, one of the grooms, no he ain't my beau, but it 's not right for women to go by themselves in the streets. My word but it was astonishing what we saw there. And they really do ride on elephants. I felt sorry for the tigers when I saw the skins of the ones that they had shot til Edward said that the tigers eat the natives and poor Sir Edward had his arm bitten off by a tiger but is still a soldier. It made feel quite faint for a moment so Eddie had to get me some cordial water. Then he held my hand. He said it was to reassure me, but I know his game.

Amelia was right to a certain extent in that I knew a great deal about the exhibition that she attended with Eddie, but not in the way that she supposed. We were worried that the Emir of Afghanistan's nephew was to visit it, for we thought that this was a ruse for the Russians to use him to contact possible insurgents in London. I was therefore sent to London ostensibly to assist with the care of the native craftsmen from India, but in reality to keep an eye on the Emir of Afghanistan's nephew.

Before I left for England I was called on by John Tyler who told me that he was also going to England and hoped to see Her Majesty while he was there. He made me send away the servants despite the fact that he knew that they would eavesdrop. He was peeved at how the man that he had chosen to be a simple waiter had risen so far and so fast. As I have so frequently found with these Chee chees they are quick to imagine that they are being slighted. Many of them are actually really quite clever. I suppose it's the European strain in their background that accounts for this trait. The pity is that they are increasingly being ignored. The white man sees them as half-breeds and the blacks as traitors. John waited until we were alone and then began:

"It's not as if he has any real ability. I grant you he has an easy manner, or used to have, for I hear that he has become somewhat proud of his dealings with Her Majesty. I mean to see someone in authority I can tell you to see if I can tell them that Abdul should never have been given the CIE. I mean to tell the truth. He's a low fellow. Only earned a few rupees when he was here working in the prison you know. Now he's being manipulated by someone. I suspect it's that Rafiuddin. He's another jumped up Indian who thinks that because he has a degree he's equal to any Englishman. The stuff he writes in those magazines..."

I listened patiently. After all it was my job, but I had difficulty in not yawning. John looked at me sharply when he had finished his diatribe and I sensed that despite my adherence to the principle that I should note everything that anyone told me I had missed the end of John's little speech.

"Well. Yes, I can certainly see your point of view."

This produced a smile of triumph. I went on cautiously like a man in a fog negotiating a glacier.

"However..."

"However what?"

"You don't want to upset Her Majesty. I understand that she has the highest regard for you."

He looked at me suspiciously.

"And where did you get that information?"

I tapped my nose and said:

"Come now John. We have known one another long enough for you to know that I have my sources."

He humphed dismissively as he looked for his umbrella.

"By the way",

I added carelessly, as he went to leave, you might find that you too could be in line for some honour, if you are reasonably circumspect."

No humph this time. A big smile instead.

We did not meet while we were in London. I was busy looking after the natives. I made sure that they were supplied with sufficient live sheep and goats to be killed appropriately so that they could eat according to their religions. Everyone knew that I was something of an expert on these matters so no awkward questions were asked about my presence. At the same time I liased with the police over the Emir of Afghanistan's nephew.

He certainly went on a number of occasions to the exhibition and I made sure that whenever he did so I was there. When we knew that he was elsewhere I was free to enjoy myself, so as I thought that I could safely leave Abdul to his work, I took the opportunity to see "The Importance of Being Earnest' and I must say that the playwright that I had met briefly in 1866 had improved enormously and looked to have a most successful career ahead of him. Little did I know of the storm that was to break over *his* head.

And I was also wrong about leaving Abdul to his own devices. He had managed to indulge himself in the worse way possible, so contacting a certain disease that nearly spoiled everything. It was Joan Biddlecome who made sure that I received all the sordid details. She said that I ought to know about my protégé. Despite her being of the fair sex she exhibited an unhealthy interest in an aspect of life that I consider should be unknown to ladies.

Abdul was to all accounts and purposes happily married. There were no signs of any children yet, but I confidently expected that there would be some in due course. I naturally assumed this without any real evidence; something that I really should not have done. Joan reported that in fact, far from being contented, Abdul had sought to indulge his normal male desires through visiting establishments that exist in plenty throughout India, and there he had been infected. I will not delineate the details that Joan had included in her report.

Suffice to say that it was the type of disease that men ran the risk of catching from women who offered themselves to men in such low establishments. Joan went further and asserted that even men who were happily married would take themselves off on occasions to such places. I am at a loss to say where she obtained such information; it might indeed be accurate, but surely no real lady would have an inkling of such behaviour still less impart a comment upon it?

My adventures in native dress gave me all sorts of insights into all sorts of people and situations as I gradually became more adept at disguising myself. Most people see what they expect to see and I found that even when they had doubts about me I could often dispel them with an appropriate comment. I usually passed myself off as a half- caste having found this satisfied most inquisitive people.   This had a double usefulness for it explained my unusual colouring and it also meant that many shunned me who might otherwise have seen though me. I had one near disaster however that was more to do with a young woman's disaffection with her husband than my failure to look other than white.

She, the young woman, set out to seduce me, and as my efforts to deceive were usually directed at men I now had to make an extra special effort at deception. In the past women in Indian society, with certain notable exceptions, were kept in the background; now life was changing, particularly in the cities. This meant that I could not avoid them. Of course I knew that in many Indian homes it was the grandmother who directed all the activities of the household, ordering about, not only her husband, but also any one else, servant or relative. She might have been out of sight but you often heard her shrill voice upbraiding all in pursuit of her dominance of those who made up her small world.

I was travelling along with many others and was a witness to one of those accidents that always seem to cause so much noise and confusion. A wheel had come loose from a bullock cart and it had tipped over sideways shedding its load of green mangoes. Small boys appeared whose manifest intention was to steal what they could while the driver, the farmer who was taking them to market, wrestled to free his bullocks. At first I watched, then as others helped the farmer I ran up and drove off the dirty bare-footed brigade of little thieves with my lathe who ran off jeering at me. My success was more due to their surprise at my intervention than anything. It was also due to the fact that the bullocks that were lowing piteously to add to the racket were soon on their feet and this meant that the farmer was able to assist me to rout them and to load his mangoes once again. I helped him. Once done he spoke:

"A thousand thanks brother."

I replied with a suitable proverb. He then swore by all his gods including Ganesh, Shiva, Rana, Suriya and Kali that those boys were no more than devils from Gehennah. I agreed. I also agreed to go with him to the market to help him in case they returned. After he had sold all his fruit he invited me to eat with him unless my caste forbade such action. Sitting together we ate the vegetable curry that he bought. I could easily have bought my own but I knew that he wanted to reward me so I held my peace and ate what he had bought.

As his way back home coincided with the way I had to go, I begged that I might sit at ease in place of the mangoes and was granted my wish. As we sat together bumping and creaking along, I related the same story about my deserting father and dying mother that I had used before so that when we reached the farmer's house, that was really no more than a mud hut, he offered me a nights accommodation. Under the sharp eye of his young wife he dragged a charpoy out into his courtyard where I had a primitive wash that at least removed the dust before I laid myself down on it to look at the stars in the warm smoky night. I lay at ease smoking a foul cheroot wondering how I was to get into the city in the morning when I heard a rustling noise.

I sat up and wrapped my pugarree around my left arm and felt for my knife with my right, only to find that the noise that I had heard was the sound of the young wife's sari. She had wrapped a scarf around her bangles so I knew that she had come to me secretly. I shall not detail what she did in order to lead me astray but I resisted her blandishments and thought that I had succeeded in resisting her. Then as she turned away I moved and my watermans fell onto the hard earth. In a moment she had picked it up and said:

"What is this? Are you a thief that you have a sahib's timepiece? "

I tried to tell her that it was mine. She said scornfully:

"Oh no! You are a thief and I will tell the constable. You are too poor to own such a treasure...unless you are a sahib."

She made no move to leave so I knew that I was beaten. Were she to go to the constable I would have to admit who I really was.

"Oh moon of delight, give me my watch and we will talk of I how might please thee."

She sat beside me and said:

"Four years have I been married to that old fool who thinks more of his fruit in the fields that the fruit of his loins. I want a son and thou shall be the means that I get one."

As she said this she undid her sari and dangled my watch before me.

I got my watch back, but I never knew if she got her son for I made sure never to go into or near that province again.

Chapter 27

1896

The truth may be the truth, but that does not mean that everyone wishes to hear it

Amelia sent me another one of her chatty letters. This one was from Balmoral. After telling how they all try to keep warm in the highlands she went on:

It was only yesterday that I was sent in to clear up the queen's study. What a mess. I have never seen it looking like that before. It looked as if some one had thrown all the papers and pens and so on onto the floor. I knew that something was up for I had heard that there had been a meeting and the rumour was that Dr Reid was going to lead a group to complain about the Moonshie to her Majesty to try to get him O U T.

There were broken ornaments on the floor and bits of glass. I gathered them all up and did my best to leave it as it should be. I could not imagine that her Majesty and Dr Reid had had a row and I was right. It was that calm Lady Harriet Phipps. Actually she ain't a proper lady, just a Lady of the Bedchamber, they still use all these odd titles. Anyway, the word is that there is something wrong with the Munshi, something so wrong that everyone don't want to sit near him. It must be something awful. Ii don't affect me of course cause he wouldn't let me sit next to him if I wanted to, and I don't ! The upshot was Lady Harriet Phipps was told by the others that she had to their dirty work and tell her Majesty. That's what caused her majesty to sweep everything all over the place. She must have been right upset.

The strange thing is that all the men seem to know what is going on but they ain't letting on. Even Eddie wouldn't say nothing to me. He said that it was better that I didn't know...

Well I suppose it could not be kept totally quiet although quite what Dr Reid thought he was up to in telling everyone that he was treating the Munshee for the effects of venereal disease I cannot imagine, unless this was a cunning ploy. to generate such a head of feeling that someone would take it into their heads to make an issue of it? In fact I heard in time that that was exactly what happened and the upshot was a very disturbed queen. What is of most interest is the way in which she still supported her favourite despite his having a social disease. She is a curious mixture. On the one hand she is so particular about protocol, whilst on the other hand being ready to flout it with John Brown and now my Abdul.

In fact what I was coming to see is that Her Majesty was not as clever as she imagined herself to be. I know that my comments are lese majeste, but as this document is extremely unlikely ever to be widely distributed, let alone published, I can safely express my opinions. With Albert at her side she was able to stand up to those toads, the politicians who profess their concern for the country but are busy at every turn lining their pockets. One only has only to see their town and country houses to establish that fact. Yes. I know that we lined ours in India, but these toads were stealing from their own countrymen, it ain't the same thing at all.

Now with Albert gone she has had to struggle alone, so it is no wonder that she turns to other men, not women you notice, they really do not have the capacity to understand how the world works, for support. So why, you might ask, does she not rely upon her own staff members? There are plenty of men, many au fait with all that is going on. I think that the answer is simply that they are courtiers in the worst sense of the word. They have not in the past spoken out, so now she no longer trusts them. Why otherwise is she ready to listen to Abdul?

I have to set out here something that troubled me intensely at the time, and as time has passed and I am older and wiser I have to admit that I am still troubled by it. It is said that the Indian Rope Trick, where a small boy climbs a rope that stays impossibly rigid when thrown in the air, is carried out by the performers by somehow making the onlookers see something that is not actually there. I have read something about Mesmer and Charcot because Joan made me do so; she called it 'educating me beyond my capabilities', one of her jokes I suppose.

At first I was sceptical. Then, as I read more, I thought that there really was something behind these ideas, strange as they seemed to be when one first examined them. I certainly discounted the theories of some form of animal magnetism, although magnetism certainly exists. I tried to keep an open mind but I did notice that those persons who seemed to be most ready to succumb to hypnosis were women, which fact did not surprise me. Having noticed this fact I decided to draw Joan's attention to it only to find that, while she encouraged my education her openness of mind was somewhat limited. Indeed, she not only lost her temper when I raised the matter, but declared that she was not going to discuss it any further with me.

So when I read: 'On the Cause of Lucid Sleep' by

by a certain Abbé Faria who had lived in Goa before going to France where it was published, I blessed the fact that I could read French and said nothing about it to Joan. She might have been interested in the fact that Abbé Faria had upset the authorities in France, and because of this he had been sentenced to a term of imprisonment in Le Chateau D'If; but if she chose to be blinkered about women and hypnotism, I was not going to say another word. You see, I knew that she had read 'The Count of Monte Cristo' by Dumas, the father, in its original French soon after it came out in 1844. This was obviously where Alexander Dumas got the idea for 'The Count of Monte Cristo'. One has to admire authors who take real situations and make up novels about them, but back to Abbé Faria's great work.

'On the Cause of Lucid Sleep' was no novel. It was instead a well-argued treatise, based upon acute observation of real cases where the Abbé Faria came to the conclusion that the effects of hypnotism come entirely from the subjects themselves.

From what I read I began to see how a mind, especially one as fine and acute as mine, could not be influenced in such a fashion. For example I must admit that I have several times been quite sure that I have observed something only to realise that it was a trick of the light that misled me. What seems to be important in situations of this kind however is the willingness of the person concerned to be so influenced. But on the occasion that I am now going to describe I do not think that I was in the least part in a state of willingness to accept what I saw and heard. I cannot tell you anything to explain it. I was not tired, nor was I drunk or under the influence of some noxious substance or drug such as opium. Neither was I ill. Certainly I was not inflamed with a touch of fever. I had eaten nothing to upset me, nor was I so hungry that I was producing visions as some ascetics do when they have starved themselves. I was in effect totally awake and in possession of all my senses when I was out alone and riding along a deserted track.

I have since talked with several Indian sages and old 'Indian hands' all of whom have accepted without question my story, having themselves either experienced similar occurrences or knew others who had. But none could offer me any explanation for what I had experienced.

As I said, I was riding alone on a waler that I had recently bought when something made look back behind me. There on a tattoo was a bareheaded woman coming up fast. It was Mrs Bollen! She was smiling, and as she passed me she called out:

"Mr Driscoll, Mr Driscoll, Oh! I am so glad."

"So glad about what?" I asked

"Why are you glad?"

She shouted out to me over her shoulder:

"It's true, it really is."

I shouted in exasperation:

"What is true?"

And I spurred my horse to catch up with her for she had gone round the corner out of my sight. When I did get there was no one to be seen. The track that ran straight for some hundreds of yards was empty. I galloped like fury along it but there was no trace of her. How could there be? I had seen her dead and buried in England; she could not be here in India.

This was no transient trick of the light. I really saw Mrs Nicola Bollen, and I heard her too. She was just as I remembered her and her voice was the one that I remembered for it had the same impatient note to it that it often had when she spoke to me. I knew that she was dead, but all I could think about was why was she here in India?

I suppose that to make this incident really interesting I should now relate some matter where her words and her appearance to me made sense of some situation. But there is nothing further that I can tell you. The incident was then, and remains now a complete mystery to me. I was not the first, I have been assured, to be vouchsafed such an apparition, nor will I be the last. India has many mysteries of this kind. A Mystic to whom I related this tale wagged his head at me, and taking my backsheesh, said:

"You must look into your heart sahib."

He then departed before I could ask how I was supposed to do that.

Chapter 28

1897

People are not naturally either friends or enemies: friendship and enmity arise from circumstances.

As this was the Queen's diamond Jubilee year I was especially on the qui vive, for I assumed that the effect that Abdul was having upon the Queen might be reflected in the way that she dealt with India, and especially the Moslems. I obtained permission to go to England but was told to travel incognito. My persona was to be that of a retired Indian administrator.

It was suggested to me that while was in England I should use this alias to look for a house so that when I retired I had somewhere to go; so in this less than subtle way it was intimated to me that once I was no longer of any use to the department they wanted to see the back of me. With some pleasant memories of Surbiton I looked in that leafy part of Surrey for an abode that I would be able to afford. I avoided Anglesea Road at first, then I was drawn back to it, by nostalgia?

How everything had changed. The steam train that I took to London went faster and was much more comfortable. Everywhere I went the changes crowded in on me. The traffic was as bad as ever, except that there were trams to add to the hazards of the streets. I was witness to a shocking accident when a cab, whose driver was so intent on getting through the press of traffic, cut out and ran down an old man who was trying to cross Piccadilly. The force of the blow that he received threw him down smashing his head upon the granite kerb. I, and several others, ran to his aid, but we were too late to help him. We carried him away from the traffic but the body that we were carrying was already a corpse.

The policeman who arrived seemed quite unable to do anything as no one knew the details of the cab. I went on my way as saddened by this as any other deaths that I had seen.

I took the opportunity to see Amelia and we took tea together in the Strand as I wanted to give her a treat and did not mind being seen in mufti with someone of her station in life. For a servant she seemed remarkably at ease with me which fact I put down to her position in the royal household. She could have been a lady until she spoke and then revealed her origins. Nevertheless I was happy to be with her and listen to her prattling on about what it was like at Osborne House. The latest downstairs scandal was about a footman who was saying that the Munshi was preventing him from getting his deserved promotion. It seemed like a storm in a teacup until one realises that to a footman not to be promoted meant not only lack of position but loss in pay. I asked Amelia how well she knew this footman, which raised a blush and a heated denial that he was anything to her. Apparently Minnie has her eye on him and forbids any poaching!

I had kept away from the celebrations and heard from Amelia the other side of things. These occasions do make a tremendous amount of work for the staff. Every lunch or dinner or similar function has to be prepared and then everything has to be cleared up. Without any prompting on my part she told me how that black stuck-up munshi-man had paraded around as if he was as good as any of the royalty that came from India.

"You can't fool servants you know. Because we are dealing with real royalty and real ladies and gents all the time we quickly know who is jumped up. Some we don't mind. They deserve it despite only having arrived recently as it were. But there are always some who presume too much. I won't name no names. We have our ways of dealing with them never you mind how, we just have. I did hear as how some of the hindoos were jealous of the Moslems, or maybe it's t'other way round. But even gentlemen can behave like children you know. What I did hear from one of the valets was that Fritz Ponsonby had had a great 'to do' in some posh club. Now don't get no ideas about me and and no valet. And don't go asking me about him and me 'cos I ain't going to tell you nothing about him, so don't bother to ask."

All this was delivered in an exaggerated whisper as if I was being told state secrets. It was just what the household feared the Munshi was doing. I leaned forward and by so doing indicated that I was ready to hear this backstairs gossip. Amelia looked at me shrewdly and went on:

"It were a row with Lord Breadalbane. It seems that this Lord has been sucking up to that Indian what has Her Royal Highness's ear. It seems that he wants a flash job in India. Well, that really upset our Fritz, so they 'had words'. Don't ask me what passed between 'em. I don't know as I weren't there was I?"

She then delivered a final salvo against Abdul, telling me that he now had three cottages that were situated on the three royal estates.

"What I want to know is what sort of hold has this man on Her Majesty what makes her give him three, yes three cottages to live in?"

She ticked them off on her stubby fingers that were so unlike those of her mothers. Hers had been much slimmer and had made me quite hot when she had laid them on my hand that time...Amelia's voice cut through my thoughts.

"One: Karim Cottage at Balmoral, two: Frogmore Cottage at Windsor, and three: Arthur Cottage at Osborne. Now, I ask you, what servant, for he is like me a, servant, gets given three cottages? Answer me that!"

Up to now as Amelia had been passing on the gossip I had heard only general matters Now however I detected someone's actual words that Amelia was transmitting to me. Which one of the men that she affected to scorn was it, I wondered.

"Is that what Eddie asks?" I asked, trying a shot at random. She laughed out loud. Several ladies at nearby tables looked at me disapprovingly. Amelia went on in almost a whisper:

"Eddie? He ain't got no idea. If you must know, it was Fritz Ponsonby hisself.

"And how did you hear 'Fritz Ponsonby hisself' express such an idea that Her Majesty was being blackmailed?"

I had gone to far. Amelia now looked affronted. It was obvious that Amelia had somehow actually overheard a conversation.

I listened to all this with mixed feelings and knew that I would have to speak to Abdul because he was still causing trouble and that was not what we wished. I knew that I would have to let him know in due course that when he came to India the next time that we would have to meet. I signalled to our waitress and paid for our tea giving Amelia time to regain her good humour, which she did in short order; she was never one to remain upset for long. I did her the honour and courtesy of allowing her to walk along the Strand in my company for despite the difference in our stations in life I was ready to make allowances. I could see that this pleased her, as did my leave taking of her for I laid it on a bit, taking her hand in mine for example, for I really liked her a great deal, although she was only a minion.

Chapter 29

1898

A wise and prudent person is not thrown into confusion by reproach

He was full of himself as usual and repeated that they were all against him. I listened as he told me that Sir James had sent for him and had set out a great list of complaints about him and his behaviour. He had tried to say that as Sir James was only the Queen's doctor it was none of his business what he (Abdul) and the Queen did. I tried to tell him that that was a most injudicious remark, but he brushed that aside, showing me just how imperious he had become. He went on:

"Dr Reid accused me of telling lies to the Queen and said that all knew that I was an impostor. He said that I was not fit to be Secretary. Secretaries spoke and wrote good English. He said I did not. He called me two-faced, that no one respects me and that I was stealing money. He threatened me by saying that he was dealing with me but it should be Prince Louis."

I tried to calm him down but he had obviously been quite upset by the whole business despite being defended by Her Majesty. In the end I grew quite cross and reminded him sharply that were it not for me, and others, he would not be in this privileged position at all. He glowered at that, for I think he would have preferred to continue to imagine that he had risen entirely through his own efforts. No one manages anything on their own, I told him. The best achievements are those that come from co-operation. He looked sullen but I think that he accepted what I had to say. I think that it was me mentioning the others that made him see sense. Much later on I realised that he was reacting to something else.

He went back to England and I was summonsed to headquarters. I went expecting a rebuke as Abdul's behaviour was getting increasingly embarrassing to us all so I prepared myself by rehearsing what I had said to Abdul. I need not have bothered. My presence was required for quite another reason. Whilst I had been busy with my efforts to do something about Indians, there had arisen another problem about them and I was to be sent to South Africa to assist in dealing with it.

Now you must be familiar with those Boers that gave us such trouble in 1881 and 1899. Oh come now that was so recent a war that most of you, even you ladies, will be familiar with all that went on. My goodness! The way the nation behaved when Ladysmith was relieved! The English are supposed to be phlegmatic not excitable like the French, but I dare say that not a few little Englanders were brought into being that memorable night! Anyway, it wasn't the Russians this time but the Germans (all related to our own dear queen) who sent military equipment and helped the Dutch settlers to fight us.

The problem that I was supposed to deal with was a simple one and arose out of our usual inability to trust the loyal Indian troops. We use them, then treat them with disdain. I was hoping that my work with Abdul Karim would change that somewhat. In the meantime I was told that despite Indian troops wishing to be involved in South Africa there were good reasons for keeping their numbers to a minimum. Mostly it was to do with money. We did not wish to have to burden the British with more costs for a campaign that had already cost a fortune. How ironic, I thought, we have bled India in the past of so much wealth and now do not wish to spend money on them.

In fact we had quite a few Indian troops in South Africa assisting with the campaign against those Dutch farmers. In order not to upset the local natives they were not actually used in the fighting. Instead they were doing the labouring and all sorts of other non-military tasks and on the whole they were quite content with that. Then everything began to worsen. Those simple farmers began to beat us. I suspect that they were not willing to fight as an organised army but more like the Spanish did when they were occupied by Napoleon's troops. The Spanish carried on what they called the little war, Guerrilla, where they would not face the whole phalanx of well-armed troops but would harry them and then run off and not fight like men.

Well, whatever anyone has to say about the right way to wage war, they forced us to retreat to Ladysmith. They then encircled the town and that meant that the town was now under siege. When the 'powers that be' heard this in India they all started to get excited and demand that should send more troops. London tried to sit on this enthusiasm but their legs were swept from under them by Lord Roberts. As the Commander in Chief in South Africa he asked for reinforcements , including native troops to be sent from India.

Faced with this the War Office capitulated and merely said that if troops were to come from India they would have to be responsible for their own provisioning. This was a cunning ploy to keeps costs down. It allowed native troops, the sepoys to be included though; and they were sent to join the fray pretty smartish, so that by August 1899 The Indian troops that arrived in Durban were the largest number of non-white troops in the war. Just as well, said those in the know for it was appalling how many would–be British soldiers had to be rejected as not being fit enough to enlist. That was a terrible scandal and just proved to my way of thinking how the working classes looked after themselves so badly they weren't fit enough to serve their queen and country in the country's hour of need. Too much drinking and smoking by half.

When the Indian reinforcements arrived they immediately had all their weapons removed. They were told that they would not need them, as they were simply there to support the British troops. You can imagine how this was received, and this was where I came in. I was told that I was to go to South Africa and use my knowledge and language skills to ensure that the sepoys and their officers understood that by supporting the fighting troops they were in essence as important, if not more important than the fighting troops.

I did what I could and I think that when you see just what the Indians and their officers achieved we could all congratulate ourselves. A good job we did congratulate ourselves for no one else did. In fact I am sad to say that the Indians and their officers were treated very badly. It always amazed though how even when this was so the ordinary sepoy still retained his loyalty to the regiment and to the queen. You might have thought that they would have been bitter, but not a bit of it, they ignored the insults and carried on just as if no one had insulted them. I can only suppose that black sepoys, although they make good soldiers if properly led by white officers, really are quite primitive, more like children.

When I have said this to Joan she has in answer consistently drawn my attention to the vast palaces, forts, tanks and temples that exist in India. She asks whether simple child–like people could have constructed them? I admit that they are certainly evidence that some one in the past has indeed had tremendous abilities. But I tell her that what we see is the remains of a great empire which is now passed away, unlike the British Empire which goes from strength to strength to such an extent that there is no possible way that it could go the same way. I ignore her mutterings about the Roman Empire and its fall, for she is totally unwilling to accept that the Romans were not British and hardened as a result by not living in a warm climate that encouraged decadence. She forgets too that the Roman Empire only existed because of its slaves.

Normally I keep away from the front line, not from cowardice you understand, but because it ain't the place where I supposed to be. But in South Africa I had to make an exception to my usual rules as it was necessary for me to slip through the lines and get into Ladysmith. I will not dwell on the way I did this. You don't want to hear tales of derring-do. Nor will I say too much about what I had to do and whom it was essential that I saw. What I will say is that as part of my work I had to see Hector MacDonald who was now a Major General in charge of the Highland Brigade. I had heard and read all about his heroics that had led to him being received by the queen herself. My prediction that he would get himself killed had not come to pass. He had certainly shown great courage and, being lucky was still alive. Now he was laid up in his quarters as he had sustained an injury to his foot.

I should have let him know that I was there but I simply assumed that as he was laid up I could barge in. He was with a young lad, one of those who were employed as runners. He swiftly departed and I was left with a sweating uneasy man who scarcely paid attention to what I had to tell him. It made me unsettled to such an extent that I remember that I stammered out my message. I was annoyed with myself for being so gauche. He obviously did not recall me from when we had met in 1880 on that march when I heard him confess that he was married but had kept it a secret. Instead he anxiously told me that these young men were absolute bricks and that Baden-Powell was so impressed with their behaviour that he was wondering how to start a young boy's movement in Great Britain. We talked about it and I agreed that it might do wonders for the working class who needed something to improve their heath and moral fibre.

When I agreed with him he settled down and insisted that I stayed for a meal. I was loath to do so but he was insistent so I gave in and picked at something ghastly that was made tolerable by some wine that he told me was produced locally. As soon as I decently could I made off, but not before Hector shook my hand insistently saying that he knew that I understood. By now I felt something was very awry so I merely agreed, nodded to his aide and sped away to make that dangerous trip through the lines. They had laid on a diversionary skirmish for me to make it easier to slip through.

Once back with my Indians I wrote my report, handed it over and set off back to India. There I dealt with my outstanding postbag and settled down with a good cheroot and a glass of port to read Amelia's latest letter to me.

Chapter 30

1899

Hoist by his own petard

'This year for the very first time I was part of the household that went to Nice. I was told that as I had been promoted (after twenty-three years I think that I have earned it, don't you?) I would be part of the royal entourage what was to be included in the Royal trip this year. It was so exciting! I have travelled around England but never before gone abroad. I was warned not to talk to any strange men, in fact not to talk to <u>any</u> men, as if I would! In any case the one or two what did speak to me spoke in their foreign lingo or in such broken English that I could scarcely keep from laughing.

I was amazed at how everyone was so upset when the Munshee (we have to call him that-not that I have anything much to do with him, he looks straight through me as well he might for he is in daily contact with her Majesty) came and joined us from England. You would think that he was an enemy or something. I know they don't like him, but this was much more than that. If looks could kill he would have died many a time.

Amelia's letter to me could not have come at a worse time. It just added to the worries that I had which started when Raj came to me to tell me about the fact that I was in deep trouble. It was all to do with Hector MacDonald the hero who had risen through the ranks, and having been given the choice of a Victoria Cross or a commission had chosen the commission. I knew him soon after when we were together on the Kandahar march. Through the years I had watched his progress. I admired the seemingly effortless way in which he had kept rising and had no notion of the rumours that surrounded him. I say that I had no notion, but to be completely honest I think I simply chose not to hear them, a foolish thing to do for a man in my line of work. I knew that he was married and had a child. It was a secret that he had revealed to me. But in any case I got to hear about it through being in the Secret Service. He had secretly married a young girl, but because of his soldiering they had scarcely ever been together. Now he was in South Africa commanding the Highland Brigade. As I wrote earlier, I met him briefly there.

Raj told me that I was about to arrested because of my association with Hector MacDonald who would in due course be unmasked as a man with strange sexual tastes! I went straight to my superior officer who told me that he would do his best to defend me but because an information had been laid they had to act. I asked who had laid the information and was not surprised to hear that it was Forbes-Boseley.

The substance of it all was the way in which Hector was recruiting young boys in South Africa to assist in the campaign there as runners. There was talk, and this coupled with things that had been said previously about Hector meant that this was being taken seriously. Because the war with the Boers had to be won, even if it meant locking up their families in camps, there would be no action taken against Hector at the moment. As a national hero it was considered that he had to be dealt with extremely carefully. On the other hand I was not seen as being that important, so unless I did something pretty swiftly I was facing the end of my career. I expected that Hector MacDonald would simply be shuffled off somewhere obscure.

It was extremely clever of Forbes-Boseley to embroil me in this fashion, for having not succeeded in getting me in trouble before, he was now using slurs about boys instead of girls; the inference being that as I was not interested in female company I must be a ...I can hardly bring myself to put the word down upon this paper. He was also using the fact that I was not married. The best defence being attack, I went straight into action. After telling Raj what I needed, I went immediately to Headquarters. I knew that there was an incriminating file about his debts in existence on Forbes-Boseley, so I used my influence to obtain it and I went and sought him out. I called on him at his bungalow where I made sure that he was alone and then showed him the file. As I knew he would, he simply laughed which told me what I needed to know, namely that he was being protected. I warned him that I had asked the head of the Department to come to his bungalow to assist me in dealing with him.

This merely provoked more laughter.

"Come now", he said,

"You do not imagine old Charley is going to be that worried about the fact that I owe money to some old jews. He ain't that particular. You had better look sharp for I do not intend to sit here all night. I am supposed to go to dinner this evening."

I tried to keep Forbes-Boseley talking for it was essential to my plan that we should both of us be here when Sir Charles arrived. Eventually I heard the sound of a donga arriving and I heard Sir Charles' patrician tones telling the driver to wait. He came in and sat down. Forbes-Boseley continued to smile, even when I showed the folder with it's incriminating evidence within it to Sir Charles, who merely rubbed his jaw and said:

"Well I own it's not the sort of thing that we like to see, but it's hardly that important is it; surely not worth calling me to come all the way here?"

Forbes-Boseley gave his usual knowing grin and I turned away as if I was beaten, but I really turned to make sure that the actor in the next part of my play was in place. He was, and he now emerged stark naked from Forbes-Boseley's bedroom. It was the young man that Raj had first briefed on my behalf, and then had brought to the back of the bungalow in order to help him get inside.

"Now lover", he said to Forbes-Boseley, who looked thunderstruck.

"What's this? Are you going to keep me waiting all night? You know I've been dying for your..."

Here he used a rude native word for the male member of generation and shook his own suggestively. I looked at Sir Charles to see whether he knew the word. From the way his face was a dangerous shade of puce and his eyes bulged I could see that he did. Forbes-Boseley threw himself upon the boy in fury. The boy had obviously been well-briefed for he nimbly jumped out of the way saying:

"Ooh! You promised me last time no more rough stuff. By the way you still owe me for that time."

He ran into an inner room and Forbes-Boseley, bellowing like a bull, chased after him. Sir Charles and I got up and left.

He said before he did so that he could see that Forbes-Boseley was an obvious bounder who had tried to smear me with the sort of beastliness that he went in for. He went off in his donga and I got onto my pony that I had tethered nearby as if to leave as well. From within the bungalow came screams. It was our young actor putting on the show of his life. When Sir Charles was safely out of sight I doubled back smartly to rescue him, but I need not have bothered. He came rushing out with his face contorted with laughter and went off into the darkness.

Of course, nothing further happened. Nothing on the surface that is. But mysteriously the information laid on me was withdrawn and Forbes-Boseley was posted a long way away. I never saw him again. Indeed I never even heard what happened to him. I suppose like many of us he retired and is now boring someone with his tales of India as I shall be in due course if I am spared that long. Of course it all went round the bazaars. I suppose that I should have told Raj to do what he could to hush it up, after all Forbes-Boseley was a white man, but somehow I never got round to doing it.

One thing that stopped me was a letter from Amelia. It did not exactly stop me, just distracted me.

I know that you like me writing to you to say whats going on and I do enjoy writing to you but I hope that if I am open in what I say that you will be careful with my letters. I suppose that I flatter myself that you keep them, but all yours to me are safely put away and I never ever show them to anybody. I felt that I had to write to you because I was right upset yesterday when I saw Her Majesty for I think that she is not at all well and those who should know better and should be helping her are making her worse.

When I looked at her I thought about my mother how she would be 63 by now if she were to be still alive tho' as you now she ain't and I saw the queen in a different way. I thought to myself that she's really only an old lady whose not well and has lost her husband and has got sons and daughters who are such a trouble to her instead of being a support to her.

Ever since she had that fall down stairs and got a bad leg and all she has not looked well but rallies when she appears in public.

Naurally I knew about this. In fact Her Majesty had developed arthritis which made her much less able to get about so she began to be taken around in a special cart. Unfortunately this meant that she put on weight and when you added this to the fact that she never lost her appetite, inevitably she turned into a little podgy lady, but who am I to point the finger of scorn? My mirror tells me an almost similar tale!

I was just clearing up and I should have been finished only I am not so quick as I used to be. So any I was still there when she came into the drawing room. I got such a look and was told to go by an equerry, but she said No let her stay and finish. She then told them to leave her alone quite sharp. I got another look from them that meant hurry up. That Munshi was with his wife in their cottage so there was just the two of us. Suddenly she says quietly is my mother still alive?

I was never so taken aback in all my born years. She never speaks to any of us normally. I told her that I lost my ma some time ago. Then I don't rightly know what came over me for I said that she had been a widow lady like her but only had the one daughter me. Not like you I added and thought that I had overstepped it, so I said that I was sorry.

You are sorry for me, she asked? No I told her I am sorry that I may have upset you at which she sighed and said I have much more to worry about than you can do to upset me. Well, I couldn't help myself she looked so careworn so I took her hand just the same as I might have had she been my ma. Just then the door opened and I was about to let go her hand when she clutched it to her saying thank you, patted it with the other hand and let it go. I went out thinking that I didn't care if I did get into trouble. The queens no more than a troubled old lady a worried mother just like my ma had been. Of course I can't tell anyone what I done, so I had to write to you.

After that, apart from a few short letters, Amelia didn't write to me again until the queen died.

Chapter 31

1901

For in and out, above, about, below,
'Tis nothing but a Magic Shadow-show,
Play'd in a Box whose Candle is the Sun,
Round which we Phantom Figures come and go.

Well, it's all over for that Indian. And I must say theres a few here what think he got his desserts. It was amazing. Almost before the Queen was in her grave he was sent packing, and that's not all by a long chalk. I heard the whole story for everyone in the household is full of it. Talk about pigeons coming home to roost. That's not the half of it.

They went to his cottage and turned him out, just like that. They didn't stand on no ceremony. But the interesting thing is the way that they made him give over all his papers and things. Then they burned the lot. Right in front of him. It must have upset him. It would have upset me, I can tell you. What was most amazing of all tho was the queen's son was there making sure that the moonshie didn't go away with anything. I reckon that Fritz Ponsonby told the Prince everything that had been going on. How that moonshie had wormed his way into the queen's affections and was so nasty to everybody so the Prince was really angry. He can be too. He might look like a big softie, but when he gets his dander up then you best beware.

The big shame to my way of thinking was that they there just let him go home. After the way he worked on Her Majesty *who was a nice enough lady but towards the end far too trusting and ready to be bamboozed by the likes of him. Well, at least we are rid of him. Very soon it will be my turn to say goodbye to the household. It will be strange not being part of all that. I suppose I shall miss it. But everything comes to an end at sometime don't it? One thing I shall certainly miss and that is writing to you. I know you like getting my letters but I expect you will have better things to do than read my nonsense.*

Amelia's letter did not astonish me for I already knew most of what she told me for it was common knowledge. Indeed, I probably knew more about than she did for I saw the official reports on the matter. It meant naturally that our plans had come to nothing. I had fallen into the trap of thinking that Her Majesty would have lived for much longer, after all she was only seventy-two when she died.

The meeting that I was subsequently called to took place in a quiet house in Belgravia. Astonishingly I saw people there sitting together for the first time who I would have thought were totally unaware that they were all in the same organisation. It was a measure of the seriousness of the situation that we were there in this fashion. Lord X chaired the meeting which had no agenda, and although I knew there would be a note of it filed away somewhere it was not apparent who would be making that note. Once the meeting was over everyone else left, not together but discreetly so as not to attract attention.

I, and several others were asked by Colonel Macy-LLewellen to remain behind, and I must tell you that I felt pretty wretched as I thought that I was to be blamed. We adjourned to a smaller room and I waited while cigars were lit.

"Well, we failed."

Eager to get it over with, I said:

"Yes I know. I am aware of our failure. I'm sorry."

"No. You cannot know for you were not aware of our intention."

"But I was: we were to get in place an Indian who would influence public opinion for us in regard of the moslems."

"That was the overt intention that we did not mind people realising."

I sat still. Overt? What then was the covert intention I asked myself? I waited. The colonel stirred and took the cigar from his mouth, blew out a cloud of smoke and said:

Well, I might as well tell you. The real intention was to get the Queen assassinated using a high profile Indian. The shock that this would cause would be used by us to crush the emerging organisations such as the Muslim Patriotic League. It would cement our control over India. It would put a spoke in the wheel of the Indian Independence Movement and pull the rug from under that bounder Ghandi."

Assassination? I shook my head. I said:

"Surely we did not need to consider such a drastic action as murdering our queen?"

"Manfred, it was necessary. Some Indians think that they should be ruling themselves. You must know from your experience of them what a preposterous notion that is. Can you imagine what this would do to the Empire were we to lose India to a bunch of jumped up Indian lawyer wallahs?"

"Unthinkable", I agreed. "But assassination?"

"Listen Manfred. The queen was old. She had had a long and useful life. Even after her Prince Consort died and she went into mourning she lead a life that she enjoyed, being queen and Empress. She served the nation in life and would have served it in death. When her friendship with John Brown became a near scandal we decided that we had to act.

We can now tell you that this long term plan was conceived as far back as 1883 when she fell down some stairs at Windsor and a little later that chap Brown died. We firmed them up when her private secretary, Sir Henry Ponsonby, informed us that she had began work on a eulogistic biography of John Brown. He got the Dean of Windsor to read a draft and when she had written several more they got together and advised her not to publish it; they did not say as much but inferred that were it to be published it would add to the rumours that John Brown had been her lover. One or two newspapers that catered for the lower orders had even called her 'Mrs Brown'.

Mind you, she was indomitable, for even when they got all the copies of her manuscripts destroyed she insisted in getting published something about life in Scotland with a dedication to her devoted personal attendant and faithful friend John Brown.

We did everything to bring the Indians into prominence so that when one of them assassinated her the repugnance that all decent Indians felt could be marshalled to consolidate our position. We couldn't use one of the Indian princes, so we got Abdul in place. I know that you have been misled in this, but if it had happened it would also have served what you and I know still exists."

"The Russian threat", I said softly.

"Precisely."

Of course I was shocked, who would not be at such a dastardly plot. Thank God that she was able to die peacefully at Osborne House. Now when I thought about events over the last few years I began to make sense of them. That time when Abdul had gone back to deal with the land that he had been allowed to purchase and had seemed so distracted. No wonder. That must have been when it had been revealed to him the full extent of the plot and the part that he was to play in it. I wondered what pressure had been bought to bear upon him and why he had not been able to resist it. I suppose that he was told that whatever he did his family would still have the land; that would have been a powerful argument.

"How was it to be done?"

"The plan was for the assassination to be carried out when the Queen was eighty. By then she would have had her Diamond Jubilee where all the Indian Princes would have come. The whole world would have seen how she trusted and treated them so nobly. It meant that the whole world, including the loyal Indians, would be horrified at such treachery. We would have put it about that it was the disloyal Indians who were engaged in political shenanigans who were behind the plot."

"But he didn't want to do it."

"No. He refused at first. We told him that we had arranged that when he had done it we would arrest him and then, through some incompetence, he would escape."

"Maybe he did not believe you."

"Perhaps. We shall never know. We did make it clear at the very beginning what we expected from him. He said then that provided he was awarded land that went to his heirs he was prepared to follow our instructions."

"Instructions that I was not privy to."

"Precisely. It was essential that you did not know and that you should continue to support him in gaining the trust of the queen."

"Which I did."

"Yes, possibly too well. For in gaining that trust he was diverted from the real purpose of getting him into a position where we could use him."

"Use him!"

"Oh, come now Manfred, you've been long enough in this game to know that everyone is used in some way. Remember, it is all for the greater good."

I looked into the fire. I thought about 'the greater good'. I thought for a moment then decided that it was time for complete honesty. I said firmly:

"I think that it is time that I revealed to you that I am Abdul's real father."

Ignoring their incredulous looks I carried on with my explanation to set out in some detail how my wife had had a child whose countenance had persuaded me that it was not mine. In order to stop gossip, which could have destroyed her, I placed the boy with Haji Wuzeenruddi who promised to look after him as if he was his own. When I subsequently found that Abdul was indeed mine I made it my business to monitor his progress, and when it became possible, I manoeuvred him into a position of influence. I thought that I would have an extra hold over him as he was my son and this would make it easier to get him to do what we required.

Macy-LLewellen listened carefully then said gently:

"I'm sorry Manfred. It seems that throughout all this time you have been living a lie."

I looked at him. Was that not what we were all doing all the time?

"Your boy, Caroline's only child that you placed with that hospital aide, died soon after. He replaced him with the son of a convicted thug. You never saw that boy in his earlier years so when you did see Abdul later on it was impossible for you to tell that Abdul was not yours. Abdul Karim was Abdul Karim."

Waves fell onto the shore within my mind. I floated away in a sea of thought.

"Manfred!"

I looked up. I realised that having been deep in thought I had not heard what Macy-LLewellen had said. He spoke again:

"The struggle continues of course. We shall never give up India. We cannot. They would be lost without us d'ye see? If we lose India then we lose our Empire and then we shall be on the downward path to degradation."

I nodded. How could I disagree? 'The greater good'. I slipped on my coat and went out, turning up my collar against the cold. But the cold was not only the English weather that I felt outside me, but also the feeling that I now had inside that something was not there any more.

I took the train to Surbiton. They were improving all the time now. I walked to my house through the leaves that covered the pavements by the Crescent. It was just beginning to rain when got to the house. There I was welcomed by Amelia who was now no longer employed at Osborne House and had come instead to join me. She had been delighted to accept my invitation to work for me.

She was anxious to show me some china that she had been permitted to take away after the funeral of the Queen. She told me that as it had Queen Victoria's crest upon it would never be used again, and that meant the servants could choose a piece or two as souvenirs. She prattled on about how the Queen had bought the set herself when she saw it at the Exhibition in London in 1851. Bertie will soon have another lot made, I thought. Sensing that I was less than interested Amelia wrapped up the china and went quietly upstairs.

Chapter 32

1902

There was a Door to which I found no Key:
There was a Veil past which I could not see:
Some little Talk awhile of ME and THEE
There seemed---and then no more of THEE and ME.

At eighty-three I was finished with India. I was also finished with all those tasks that had taken me to all sorts of places. I felt tired each morning when I arose to face another day. How many had I left to me I wondered as I drank my morning coffee? I had been ill several times in my career and only my strong constitution and a good diet had helped me survive. Now I wanted to enjoy what was left of my retirement in Surbiton where I had a pleasant house and a modest pension that enabled me to live comfortably as a gentleman should.

I also had Amelia, for as I said previously I had asked her to come to live with me and look after my house as her mother had back in 1866. Amelia had been fourteen then, a pretty enough child, but extremely shy. Now at forty-nine she is stockier and much more self-assured. She found running my household no trouble, and gradually she moved from being a servant to being more of a daughter to me.

The other day she came to me and without any preamble said:

"You were very fond of my Ma weren't you?"

I nodded, wondering what she was going to say next. She said nothing. Instead she held out a picture to me.

"I found this among her things just after...you know."

I took it and looked at the sepia image of someone who could have changed my life and almost did so. I said nothing.

" I kept it by me ever since, but I'd like you to have it, but only of you do me a favour."

She said those last words in a hurry as if she was unsure that she ought to have said them at all.

"What favour is that?"

Suddenly she lost her composure. I saw again the young woman that had waylaid me in London, shy and unable to speak. I waited. At last she looked at me directly with those eyes that were so like her mother's and said:

"My letters. You know the ones that I wrote to you. Can I have them back please?"

"How do you know that I kept them? I teased.

She blushed and I knew that she had seen them when Agatha the new maid of all work had been ill and she had cleaned my room in her place.

"It's only, that is to say, I only feel that I..." her voice trailed away, then she took on a new look and became again the resolute woman that she had become over the years.

"It's only that I feel ashamed of them. My spelling and grammar you know and..."

"...And? I prompted.

"Well, I was hardly the soul of discretion, was I?"

I looked again at the picture of her mother who looked out steadily at me from the past. It would be a fair trade. This picture, whose existence I had only guessed at, would be worth to me so much that were I to try to put a value upon it I would fail.

"Yes, I agree. Give me some time and I will give them to you."

Yes, I know that I should not have agreed. Those letters were a remarkable record and should have been preserved in their entirety. Instead I resolved to copy those parts of them that I need for this account, and when I had done so return them to Amelia who I knew would destroy them. Far better she should destroy the letters if it meant that I could retain her mother's picture. Over the next few days I made my notes and then I returned Amelia's letters to her. They went into the fire straight away of course. I watched her do it. When she had done so I went up to my study.

I poured myself a glass of port and sat at my desk. I drew a sheet of paper towards me. Of course I knew that what I had learned over the years was secret and that it should remain so, but I resolved that I would leave a record of my part in the continuance of the struggle to maintain the Empire. But somehow after another port I lapsed into idleness. I put aside my first attempt and thought that someday I would finish it.

Then one day as Amelia was beginning to serve a meal that I insisted she should call tiffin, she asked me whether I missed India.

"Do I miss India?" I replied.

"How could I not do so?"

She poured my coffee. Its smell brought back the way in which I was woken early one morning by my bearer who very often brought a message along with it that made me get up immediately.

"How could I not miss riding out on a horse that my syce had brought round knowing that his sahib would need it immediately. How could I not miss riding like the devil with the villagers running alongside me trying to keep up as I went to shoot the tiger that had killed one of their children and was now laid up in the long grass with the child's body. I shot it as it sprang towards me. Afterwards I felt like a god. And then back to work as part of a huge administration that brought order and justice to so many: from princes to chumars; from Sunni Mullahs to kitmagars; for all, whether they are ahirs, sadhus or high caste Brahmins. Yes, it was wearisome, tedious and sometimes futile but there was *such* satisfaction on occasions.

I knew that I was losing Amelia's attention but I could not stop myself from carrying on:

Mother India! So vibrant! So surprising! And so seductive! Once you have embraced her she never lets you go you know. Her kiss poisons your blood with a sweet subtle substance that stays in your body wherever you may travel and binds you to her. Some escape, only to find that they have left their hearts behind."

I looked at Amelia who said with a smile:

"I'll get your eggs then."

I am not a vain man, but then neither am I very rich and certainly not loaded with honours, as some are who have served their country. So I decided that I would indeed write a narrative that were it to come to light in the future, then those who are administering matters in India on behalf of Great Britain would know the small part that I had in ensuring that they are still in charge of that part of our empire. I dipped my pen into the ink and began.

Authors' note- continued

Having finished reading Manfred Driscoll's manuscript I went back to the house in Anglesea Road where the present owners kindly allowed me to look in the attic. I admired the new extension that had effectively removed all traces of everything that had been there originally, keeping as blank a face as possible to mask my disappointment that there was nothing further for me. I thanked the new owners and left by the front door, where as I walked down the steps the old man across the road that I had met when the skip was still there, hailed me.

"Hello squire! I thought it was you", he said and went on to tell me that after I had taken away my bundle of newspapers he had also rummaged in the skip.

"I found these", he said holding out a cardboard box that rattled in his shaky hands.

"I offered them to the new owners but they said that that they were not interested in some dirty old china and a picture so I could keep them. I thought of you immediately and held onto them in case you came back. Do you want them?"

"Thanks", I said and took them home.

The two side plates were extremely dirty and one of them had a crack in it. I washed them carefully and was pleased to discover that they were very pretty and had Queen Victoria's cipher upon them. The photograph was of a plump youngish woman who stared severely at me. From her dress she could have been a servant but it was the bunch of keys hanging at her waist that made me think that she was a housekeeper. I turned it over. Just legible I made out the following words:

'Taken at Surbiton Park Terrace Studios
Mrs Nicola Bollen.'

There was something else written in a cursive script but it was so faded I could only make out the words 'love', 'Nicola' and 'old fool'. It seemed that rain or damp had obliterated the remainder of what had been written, or was it tears?

Note on the persons and events that appear in the story.

As I arranged Manfred Driscoll's manuscript for publishing I wondered whether I should add some notes at the end to explain who these people were about whom he wrote. I also considered adding something similar about the events that he described. I have resisted the temptation, leaving it to the readers, who either already know them, or can read about them for themselves.

Lightning Source UK Ltd.
Milton Keynes UK
UKHW011851130420
361650UK00001B/30